The Taste of Rain

Author: Monique Polak

D0376348

This novel for middle readers takes place in China in WWII, where thirteen-year-old Gwen follows the Girl Guide code in order to survive.

Format	Paperback	PDF	EPUB
5 x 7.5	9781459820265	9781459820272	9781459820289
224 pages	$10.95		

KEY SELLING POINTS:

- Based on a true story, *The Taste of Rain* tells the tale of a young girl who grapples with physical hardship and moral dilemmas while imprisoned in the Weihsien internment camp in China during World War II.

- The book features themes of loyalty, friendship, prisoners of war, making moral choices, codes of honor, and prejudice.

- This is a unique story with a vivid setting and memorable characters.

- Author Monique Polak has a special interest in researching the lives of children during World War II. Her mother was a Holocaust survivor, who spent nearly three years in a Nazi concentration camp. Her novel *What World is Left*, winner of the Quebec Writers' Federation Literature Prize, was inspired by her mother's wartime experience.

- Monique's editor heard an NPR segment about a Weihsien survivor named Mary Previte and suggested that Monique write about the Girl Guides in the camp.

- Real-life missionary and Olympic gold-medal winner Eric Liddell (depicted in the movie *Chariots of Fire*) died of cancer in Weihsien in February 1945 and is a character in the book.

ABOUT THE AUTHOR:

MONIQUE POLAK is the author of over twenty novels for kids and young adults. She has also written two nonfiction books for kids (*Passover: Festival of Freedom* and *I Am a Feminist: Reclaiming the F-Word in Turbulent Times*), as well as a board book for toddlers. Monique teaches English literature, creative writing and humanities at Marianopolis College in Montreal, Quebec. For more information, visit moniquepolak.com.

PROMOTIONAL PLANS INCLUDE:
- Print and online advertising campaigns
- Promotion at national and regional school, library and trade conferences
- Digital and print ARCs available

BISAC
JUV016030 JUVENILE FICTION / Historical / Asia
JUV039010 JUVENILE FICTION / Social Themes / Physical & Emotional Abuse
JUV039220 JUVENILE FICTION / Social Themes / Values & Virtues

RIGHTS
Worldwide

AGES
9–12

Order online at orcabook.com or orders@orcabook.com or 1-800-210-5277

@orcabook

ORCA BOOK PUBLISHERS
orcabook.com • 1-800-210-5277

The
TASTE
OF RAIN

The
TASTE
OF RAIN

Monique Polak

ORCA BOOK PUBLISHERS

Library and Archives Canada Cataloguing in Publication

Polak, Monique, author
The Taste of Rain / Monique Polak.

Issued in print and electronic formats.
ISBN 978-1-4598-2026-5 (softcover).—ISBN 978-1-4598-2027-2 (pdf).—
978-1-4598-2028-9 (epub)

Library of Congress Control Number: TO COME
Simultaneously published in Canada and the United States in 2019

Summary: This novel for middle readers takes place in a Japanese internment camp in China in WWII, where thirteen-year-old Gwen follows the Girl Guide code in order to survive.

Orca Book Publishers is dedicated to preserving the environment and has printed this book on Forest Stewardship Council® certified paper.

Orca Book Publishers gratefully acknowledges the support for its publishing programs provided by the following agencies: the Government of Canada, the Canada Council for the Arts and the Province of British Columbia through the BC Arts Council and the Book Publishing Tax Credit.

Edited by Sarah Harvey
Cover design by Rachel Page
Cover illustration by Jensine Eckwall
Author photo by John Fredericks

ORCA BOOK PUBLISHERS
orcabook.com

Printed and bound in the United States.

22 21 20 19 • 4 3 2 1

For Sarah Harvey. With gratitude, respect and love.

ONE

"Rise and shine, Girl Guides!" Miss E. calls from the doorway. "It's time to get dressed and welcome another shiny new day." Even when she isn't singing, Miss E.'s voice sounds like music.

Tilly, who is lying next to me, her shoulder bumping up against mine, covers her eyes. "I am really not a morning person," she mutters. Then she turns onto her other side and fake snores.

"Stop it," says Dot, Tilly's neighbor on the other side, blocking her ears.

I nudge Tilly. "Come on," I say. "Miss E. is right. It's time to welcome another shiny new day."

"*Shiny new* argh!" Tilly says to the ceiling. "Something tells me it won't be any better than yesterday or the day before. And I wouldn't use the words *shiny* or *new* for either of those days."

Our uniforms are folded and ready at the bottom of our sleeping pallet. I toss Tilly hers, then grab mine. Though the cotton is worn thin, and the skirt has become too short for me, I can't help smiling when I run my fingers over my newest badge: *Artist*. I think about the pencil sketch I drew of our boarding school back in Chefoo, and how much Miss E. liked it. "Why, Gwen," she'd said, "this sketch is so realistic it gives me shivers."

"I told the boys' teacher that I'd go next door and wake up the boys too," Miss E. calls. "I'll be back in five minutes for our morning prayer and song!"

"What about our pep talk?" Jeanette asks. Jeanette *is* a morning person. Her uniform is already on. Even her pale blue scarf is tied nicely around her neck.

"Yes," a girl named Cathy adds. "Don't forget about our pep talk." Cathy's scarf is still on the pallet. She is up on her tiptoes, stretching her arms over her head.

Miss E. laughs and claps her hands. "Not to worry, Girl Guides! Every shiny new day begins with a prayer, a song—and a pep talk!"

I pull the blue tunic over my head and tie on my scarf, though I can never seem to do it as nicely as Jeanette does. Even Tilly is getting dressed now, and Cathy is tying on her scarf. We can hear Miss E. outside, crowing like a rooster. The boys answer with a chorus of groans and laughter.

By the time Miss E. is back, all twenty-eight of us girls have formed two neat lines in front of our wooden sleeping pallets. Because there's so little room, we squeeze together as tightly as matches in a matchbox.

We are together when we sleep, but we spend most of our time in smaller groups. Tilly and Jeanette are my two closest friends. Then there's Cathy and Dot, who always seem to be together, and Eunice and Margaret. We are all part of Miss E.'s Girl Guide troop at Chefoo.

"Don't you girls look dapper!" Miss E. tells us. She presses her palms together over her heart, drops her head and launches into the Lord's Prayer: "*Our Father who art in heaven, hallowed be Thy name…*"

We've all said this prayer so many times the words come automatically. But I try to concentrate on what they mean. That's what Miss E. wants us to do. It's also what my parents would want. But I don't concentrate on the prayer's words for my parents. I do it for Miss E.

"*Give us this day our daily bread…*"

I should be thinking about the Lord, but instead I'm thinking about how much I'd like a slice of toasted white bread with butter and strawberry jam—and a steaming cup of Lipton tea with milk and six tablespoons of sugar.

When the prayer is done Miss E. announces she wants to teach us a new song. "You'll love it, Gwen," she says, singling me out, "because it's American. It's about a boy who plays the bugle."

Miss E. curls her left fingers and brings them to her mouth, then stretches out her right arm like she is playing a bugle.

She lowers her pretend bugle and starts to sing. *"He was a famous trumpet man from out Chicago way. He had a boogie style that no one else could play."*

Miss E. taps one foot. She doesn't need to ask us to join in. We are already playing our own pretend bugles and tapping our toes to the beat. What a fun song! And it's patriotic too. No one—not even Tilly—can be in a bad mood when she sings this song.

"He was the top man at his craft. But then his number came up and he was gone with the draft."

It's also easy to learn. My favorite part is when it goes "A-toot. A-toot. A-toot-diddelyada-toot."

Jeanette drops her pretend bugle. "What do you think *diddelyada* means?" she asks.

Tilly stops tapping. "It doesn't mean anything. It's just a sound."

We do the song three more times with the arm gestures and foot tapping—and a lot of laughter.

When she smiles, Miss E.'s gray eyes shine and her dimples show. "That was an excellent way to warm up our bodies," she says. "Even better than a cup of tea. Now for that pep talk I promised."

We sit down cross-legged on the dirt floor, elbows in so there is room for all of us. Miss E. kneels down to face us. Her face glows. I don't know if it's from the singing or the exercise or because she loves being with her Girl Guides. All three probably.

"Today," Miss E. begins, "is a wonderful gift. It may not be sunny outside, but in here"—she taps her chest where her heart is—"it is always warm and sunny, never muggy." That makes us laugh. It's May, and the weather in northern China is already unbearably muggy, making it even harder for us to fall asleep at night. It's almost bad enough to make a person look forward to February, when it's so cold our hands and feet get blisters.

"We are together," Miss E. continues. "And we are so grateful for that. Together we shall continue to make the most of this day and every day the Good Lord sees fit to give us. And today, like every day, as Girl Guides you must all find a way to do a good turn for someone—without any expectation of reward. How was that pep talk?" There is laughter in Miss E.'s eyes.

We answer by applauding.

"Well then," Miss E. says, "let's recite the Girl Guide Promise."

Even Tilly, who is looking more awake, joins in.

I promise, on my honor, to do my best:
To do my duty to God, the Queen, and my country,
To help other people at all times,
And to obey the Guide Law.

Just as we finish reciting the promise, a fat gray rat scurries across the dirt floor. Jeanette shrieks. Tilly groans.

Dot and Cathy whimper. Several girls grimace. We should be used to the rats by now. Just like we should be used to the bedbugs and the lice. But the last thing we want is any more roommates.

For a split second even Miss E. looks alarmed, but then she bursts into laughter. "Did you see that fellow's whiskers?" she asks. "Why, he's the spitting image of my uncle Edward. Minus the glasses, of course. Did I ever tell you about my uncle Edward? He was a chemist. He knew all about herbs."

A chemist who knew about herbs? I'd like to hear more about him, but Miss E. is already on to another topic. She has the kind of brain that jumps from topic to topic, then back again. Tilly gets annoyed by Miss E.'s way of thinking, but I love it. I have loved every single thing about Miss E. since my first day at the boarding school in Chefoo, where she was our head teacher and Girl Guide leader.

"One of these days I'm going to show you girls how to trap a rat," Miss E. is saying. "We'll make it a game. You can compete with the other children from Chefoo. With 140 of you, we could have many teams. The team that traps the most rats on a given day shall win a prize."

"A prize?" we call out. What kind of prize is Miss E. thinking of?

"Absolutely," Miss E. says. "What's a game without a prize?"

When we hear footsteps outside our hut, Miss E. brings one finger to her lips and winks at us. "Company's coming," she whispers.

We stand up, shoulders back, eyes forward.

"*Kiwotsuke*," the Japanese soldier barks as he strides into our hut. *Kiwotsuke* is one of the first Japanese words we learned after the Japanese invaded China. It means "at attention." The soldier's right hand is on the shiny sword he wears at his side. He scans the hut, the pallets, all twenty-eight of us, before his eyes land for a brief moment on Miss E. Some of the Japanese soldiers are nicer than others. This one's eyes are cold, and his face shows no feeling. He is not tall, and he has a thin black mustache.

Miss E. smiles, but her dimples don't show. "*Ohayo gozaimasu*," she says, which means "good morning" in Japanese. This time her voice doesn't sound musical.

The Japanese soldier clicks the heels of his black knee-high boots together, then turns his back on us and leaves our hut. When he pushes on the door, I see a strip of gray sky and, in the distance, a watchtower. If I squint, I can see another soldier standing inside the tower, his rifle extended like a sword. Though the day is already steaming hot, I shiver.

Miss E. claps. "*Ohayo gozaimasu*," she says to all of us.

"*Ohayo gozaimasu*," we answer in one voice.

"Your Japanese is getting awfully good, Guides," Miss E. says. "Now how about joining me in another round of 'Boogie Woogie Bugle Boy'?"

TWO

We have been imprisoned at Weihsien for almost two and a half years.

On December 8, 1941—the day after the Japanese attack on Pearl Harbor—the Imperial Japanese Army took over our boarding school in Chefoo. They affixed Japanese seals to every single piece of furniture—even the chalkboards in our classrooms—and forced all of us students, and even our teachers, to wear red armbands. Mine has the letter *A* on it because I am American, though I have lived in China since I was three. Tilly, whose family comes from Britain, has a *B* on hers.

For a year we lived like prisoners in our school. Because our parents are missionaries working in inland China, they were too far away to help us. When the Japanese decided they needed our boarding school for military operations, we were taken by steamer and then by train to the Weihsien

Civilian Assembly Center in northern China. Civilian assembly centers are what the Japanese call places like these. What they really are is prisons.

Miss E. once asked us to try imagining what Weihsien was like ages ago, when it was an American Presbyterian compound with pretty brick houses, a real school and hospital and lush green gardens. That took a lot of imagination. Even before it was turned into a prison, Weihsien was looted by Chinese bandits, then occupied by Japanese soldiers. None of them took very good care of the place.

Now the buildings are falling down, the gardens are overgrown, and the roads are strewn with rubble and leftover bits of broken furniture that will be used for firewood next winter. The school's been turned into a dormitory, and the hospital has hardly any medicine. Worst of all, eighteen hundred prisoners have to share only twenty-three toilets, which seldom flush, since we get so little water. The only buildings that aren't falling down are the ones where the Japanese soldiers live and work. Most of those are at the back of the camp, in an area we're not allowed to enter.

I will never forget how, when we arrived at Weihsien in 1942, Miss E. pointed to the three Chinese characters inscribed over the gate at the main entrance. "Le Dao Yuan," she said, reading the characters to us. "That means 'Courtyard of the Happy Way.' Isn't that lovely? And we shall make every effort, Girl Guides, to be happy in this place. Won't we, Girl Guides?"

Of course, we'd all agreed. Only back then we didn't know how hard life at Weihsien would be, nor how long we'd be here.

It was Miss E.'s idea to pack our Girl Guide uniforms along with textbooks, games and art supplies. The other teachers went along with the plan, not only because Miss E. was head teacher, but also because she convinced them that if we followed the Girl Guide code, life in a prison would be easier to bear.

There is no white toast, strawberry jam, Lipton tea or sugar at Weihsien.

All we get for breakfast is a bowl of boiled broomcorn mush. Until we came here, I never knew that people ate broomcorn. Back in Chefoo, which is on the country's eastern coast, the farmers fed broomcorn to their cows, chickens and ducks. The women made brooms from the broomcorn grass. Which explains the name broomcorn.

Broomcorn doesn't taste very good, but when your stomach is so empty it feels hollow, and there's nothing else for breakfast, broomcorn does the trick.

We line up to get our broomcorn in one of the camp kitchens—there are four of them—with plates and spoons we brought from Chefoo. Mine and Tilly's aren't exactly plates; they are small cast-iron frying pans. Another prisoner ladles out the broomcorn—a scant half ladle for each of us. She is so thin her cheekbones poke out of her face, and her lips, like all of ours, are dry and cracked from lack of water.

Some people get into arguments. Yesterday a man complained he didn't get enough of the grainy mush. Another day, two grown-ups waiting in line shoved each other. A Japanese soldier broke things up by grabbing hold of the two people and slamming them together so hard we heard their foreheads crack.

Miss E. does not tolerate arguing or complaining from any of us. Girl Guides mind their manners at all times. Or as Miss E. puts it, "It doesn't matter whether you're at Buckingham Palace or the Weihsien Civilian Assembly Center. Good manners are a constant."

Miss E. announces that she has a special treat for us this morning. It is something in a bowl, and because I can see Miss E.'s tin spoon poking out from her apron pocket, I am hoping it will be food. Maybe oatmeal. Or if I could choose anything at all, spicy soup with slices of sweet pork in it, the kind of soup we got sometimes in Chefoo.

"Come see what I have for you," Miss E. tells us. "It's for your health. To maintain your bones."

When Miss E. says that, I decide there's no oatmeal or spicy soup in her bowl.

There's a pasty whitish mixture in it.

"Is it candy?" Jeanette asks hopefully.

"Of course it isn't candy. Whoever heard of candy paste?" Tilly rolls her eyes.

"Now, now." Miss E. gives Tilly a sharp look. "A Girl Guide is a friend to all and a sister to every Guide. It's the fourth Girl Guide law."

"I'm sorry," Tilly says to Jeanette, but if you ask me, Tilly doesn't sound too sorry. Maybe because she wants to make up for being snappy, Tilly offers to have the first spoon of the mysterious paste.

"What is it anyhow?" Tilly asks before she opens her mouth.

"A better question," Miss E. says, "is what you'd *like* it to be. If it could be anything in all the world, what would you choose, Matilda?"

Tilly closes her eyes while she thinks about her answer. "English toffee," she says when she opens them again. Tilly thinks everything from Britain is best—especially the people who live there.

"Well then, English toffee it is. Open your hatch," Miss E. says.

Tilly opens her mouth wide. She makes a gulping sound and winces as she swallows the stuff. There's some whitish paste left on her lips. The pupils of her eyes get very big, and she sputters and coughs like a train engine that is about to die. "Ugh," she says, spitting out whatever is left in her mouth, "that is the yuckiest thing I ever tasted. It's nothing like English toffee."

Miss E. sighs. "I should never have let you go first," she tells Tilly. "Now how will I ever get the other girls to take it?"

I'm not used to hearing Miss E. sound discouraged.

"I'll go next," I offer.

"Why, that's very kind of you, Gwen. I suppose I might as well tell you what's in this paste. I went to a lot of trouble to get it. It's crushed eggshells mixed with a little fresh water. It was almost as hard to get my hands on the fresh water as it was to get the eggshells."

"Crushed eggshells?" Tilly says. "Are you saying I just *ate* crushed eggshells?"

"You certainly did. They're excellent for you. Full of calcium," Miss E. says.

Tilly puts her hands on her hips. "In that case, why don't *you* take a spoonful yourself?"

Cathy, who is next in line after me, says, "Yes, why don't you? You can have my turn, Miss E."

Tilly always says what's on her mind, and Cathy usually agrees with Tilly.

"It's more important for you children to have it." Miss E. drops her voice. "Your bones are still growing."

Your bones are still growing. Her words remind me of when I was little and lived with my parents. It would have to have been before 1939, when they left me at the boarding school in Chefoo so they could do their missionary work.

Mother used to make me take a spoonful of cod liver oil before bed. "Your bones are still growing," she'd say. Just the smell of cod liver oil made me want to vomit. Mother showed me the trick of pinching my nose before I swallowed it.

For a moment I feel a giant longing for my parents. I haven't seen them for so long that I thought I'd gotten over missing them. I can hardly remember the sounds of their voices. *Your bones are still growing.*

Some people might say it's selfish of us to miss our parents, since they are doing God's work, converting nonbelievers to Christianity. But sometimes I think that looking after your own child is more important than any other work—even God's. I have decided that if I ever have a child, I will never leave her to go and help some strangers. I will always put her first.

"Ready, Gwen?" Miss E. asks.

I take a deep breath and open my mouth.

"Down the hatch!" Miss E. says as she puts the spoon of paste into my mouth.

I nearly gag. The taste is as bad as Tilly said it was. But I close my eyes and swallow it down. I even lick my lips.

I smile up at Miss E. When she smiles back I forget the bad taste. Miss E.'s smile tells me she is grateful that I've made her job a little easier.

THREE

Miss E. believes in routine. That's why, every morning after broomcorn, she makes her students from Chefoo sweep out their huts. "Cleanliness is next to godliness," she says, pointing to a cobweb Eunice has missed in the corner and smiling approvingly when the cobweb is gone.

Miss E. says routine brings comfort, and that when life presents challenges, routine helps steady a person. Miss E. says we are all like boats sailing on an ocean with waves that can get dangerously big. Routine helps us ride the waves and keep floating.

Jeanette is humming "Boogie Woogie Bugle Boy."

Tilly, who along with several other girls is using a knife to dig bedbugs out of the mattresses on our sleeping pallet, sighs. "Could you keep it down?" she says to Jeanette. "Or better still, could you stop humming altogether? You're giving me a headache."

Cathy looks up from squashing a bedbug. "Me too," she says.

Jeanette stops humming. "Sorry," she whispers to the two girls. I think Jeanette is a little afraid of Tilly. To be honest, we are all a little afraid of Tilly. All of us except for Miss E., of course. Miss E. is not afraid of anyone—not even the fiercest of the Japanese soldiers. When I grow up I want to be as brave, beautiful, wise and cheerful as Miss E.

Daily lessons are also part of our routine here. When we've finished cleaning and Miss E. has inspected every inch of the hut, she reaches into her apron pocket for her reading glasses. At boarding school a bell rang when it was time for class. We don't need a school bell at Weihsien. When Miss E. puts on those glasses, lessons are about to begin.

We sit on the steamer trunks we brought from Chefoo. Even if we don't have chairs, desks or a chalkboard, we can still learn.

Today Miss E. is teaching us geography. "The Yangtze River is the longest river in all of Asia." She spreads out her arms on the word *longest*. "You should probably jot that down in your notebooks."

I raise my hand. "Miss E.," I say, "I'm at the end of my notebook. Are there any extras?"

Miss E. shuts her eyes. She does that when she is trying to solve a problem. There must not be any extra notebooks.

"I'm nearly at the end of mine too," Jeanette adds.

"Me too," Dot and Cathy say at the same time.

Tilly shakes her head. "I still have lots of pages." She uses her index finger to count the number of pages she has left. "Seventeen! You three must have made your letters too big." From her tone you'd think Tilly's the teacher and we're *her* class.

Miss E. opens her eyes and claps. "I've got a solution." She reaches into her apron pocket and pulls out a rubber eraser. "Ta-da," she says, holding the eraser out in front of her. "You girls must erase every single thing you've written in your notebooks."

"Every single thing?" Judging from the way she's raised her eyebrows, Jeanette does not like Miss E.'s plan.

"Every single thing," Miss E. says. "Then it'll be like having a brand-new notebook!"

Dot looks like she's about to cry. Dot always looks like she's about to cry. "If we erase everything in our notebooks," she asks, "how will we remember all the things you've taught us? A person needs notes to remember things. Isn't that why you always tell us to jot things down?"

This time Miss E. doesn't have to close her eyes to come up with an answer. "Take it from me, Girl Guides, you'll remember our lessons in here." She taps the side of her head three times. "Besides, the very act of writing things down—of moving your pencil along a blank page—is a way of remembering."

Miss E. hands me the eraser first. It feels a little sad to erase the notes from the lessons we learned in our first days at Weihsien, but I'm sure Miss E. is right. She's always right. I'll never forget everything she's taught us.

"Before the days of steam engines," Miss E. continues, "men called trackers had to pull ships by hand up certain sections of the Yangtze River."

"Did women work as trackers too?" Tilly forgets to raise her hand.

"That's a good question, Matilda. I believe the trackers were mostly men. A woman would have to be very strong to help pull a ship up a river," Miss E. says.

Cathy raises her hand. "You're always telling us girls can do anything boys can do."

"Indeed," Miss E. says. "Well then, there may well have been women trackers too. Only they may not have made it into our history books."

"That isn't fair," Tilly says.

"Quite right," Miss E. says.

There is a loud rapping on the door to our hut. It's one of the older boys from Chefoo. He doesn't wait for Miss E. to invite him in.

We groan when we see what the boy is carrying—a fat dead rat.

I know it's dead because of the way the rat's head sags to one side and the glassy look in its beady eyes.

Jeanette scrunches her eyes shut. "Tell me when he's gone," she whispers to me.

"Do you mean the boy or the rat?" I ask her.

"Both," Jeanette says without opening her eyes.

"It's for the rat-catching contest!" the boy announces. He has sandy-colored hair. His face, like everyone's at

Weihsien, is pale and terribly thin. Maybe that's why his dark, lively eyes stand out. "We clubbed him to death."

Miss E. does not blink at the sight of the dead rat. "Matthew," she says to the boy, her voice as calm as it was when she was teaching us about the Yangtze River, "I appreciate your enthusiasm. But I'm afraid you've interrupted our geography lesson."

FOUR

All this leads to a loud debate about the murder of rats.

Tilly is in favor. "Rats are filthy creatures."

Cathy is in favor too. "Didn't they spread the Plague during the Middle Ages? What if we catch the Plague?" she asks.

"I don't think there's much danger of that," Miss E. says. "In fact, I read that it wasn't rats who spread the Plague—it was people. Which is why, whenever there is boiled water available, I'm always telling you girls to wash your hands. So that you don't catch dysentery, which is a far bigger problem around here than the Plague."

Jeanette says every living creature has a soul and it's a sin to club a rat to death. "Couldn't we just catch them and let them out somewhere else?" she suggests.

"If we did that, they'd find their way back—and they'd be scuttling across this floor the next day," Tilly tells her.

Miss E. closes her eyes for a moment, then opens them again. "Unless, of course, we released the rats outside Weihsien…"

"How could we do that?" Tilly says. "We're prisoners here."

"There is always a way," Miss E. tells Tilly. "And—I don't know why I never thought of this before—we should try to come up with a nicer-sounding word than *prisoner*."

"We *are* prisoners," Tilly says flatly. "It's the right word."

I watch the two of them carefully. In all the time we have known her, none of us has ever dared talk back to Miss E. I wonder what she'll do. I predict Miss E. will find a way to reprimand Tilly. Miss E. is very firm when she has to be.

But Miss E. does something that surprises me. She smiles. "I prefer the word *sojourners* to *prisoners*," she says. "It has more possibility. *Sojourner*," she says again, as if she's trying out the word and likes the sound of it. "A sojourner never stays anywhere very long."

Tilly rolls her eyes.

Some of the other girls like the sound too, because they start tossing the word around like a bouncing ball.

"Hello, *sojourner*!" Eunice says to Margaret.

"Did you just call me *sojourner*?"

"As a matter of fact I did, *sojourner*."

Miss E. says she knows a way to catch a rat without killing it. "We'll need a bucket and two narrow strips of wood. And something for bait."

"Maybe we can use a ruler for one of the strips," Jeanette suggests. "There's a wooden ruler in the trunk with our school supplies."

Miss E. thinks the ruler is a good idea. "I need a volunteer to go to the latrine to fetch a bucket. And someone else to go and find another strip of wood—a touch longer and wider than a ruler."

Jeanette has opened the trunk and is looking for the ruler. Tilly says she'll find another strip of wood. It's up to me to get the bucket.

The latrine is a short way down a gravel path from our hut. When the wind blows the wrong way, the stink is so strong we can taste it.

I pinch my nose as I get closer. That reminds me of the cod liver oil again. What, I find myself wondering, are my parents doing this second? Are they teaching Bible studies or helping a family in need? I doubt they're thinking about me. If they'd thought of me in the first place, they'd never have left me behind in Chefoo when I was only seven.

But wouldn't it be a coincidence if we really were thinking about each other at the very same time? My parents can't have completely forgotten me. I'm their only child, after all. Why didn't they have the good sense to leave China before the Japanese invasion? There had been many rumors about the threat of invasion and the cruelty of the Japanese. How could my parents have been so foolish?

There's a row of tin buckets on the low steps leading to the latrine. The ones called honeypots are kept inside the huts overnight so prisoners—excuse me, I mean *sojourners*—can pee without having to walk all the way here. Others are for scrubbing the latrine floors. I pick up the closest bucket and sniff it. The bucket stinks of urine—and worse—so I grab another.

"What are you doing with that bucket?" a man's voice asks in halting English.

When I look up I see knee-high black boots and khaki-colored pants. Why didn't I notice the Japanese soldier standing on guard by the latrine? This one has a round face and big ears.

"We need it to catch rats. We're going to have a cont—" I stop myself. Then, because I am remembering how friendly Miss E. always is, even to the Japanese, I try giving the soldier a small smile.

He does not smile back. I worry he'll punish me. Catching rats may not be a crime, but many of the Japanese soldiers are very harsh and cruel. During roll calls they often shout at prisoners. Anyone who is slow to line up gets two hard slaps to the face, one to each cheek. I've even seen soldiers remove their belts and use them to strap prisoners for moving in their spots. Once I saw a Japanese soldier stuff a rag into an old man's mouth so he wouldn't be able to scream while he was being strapped. It was the saddest thing I ever saw.

What if this soldier stuffs a rag into my mouth and straps me?

He studies my face. Then his eyes drop down to my pale-blue scarf, my Girl Guide uniform and my worn-out leather shoes. Because they've gotten so tight, I keep the laces loose. A few weeks ago Miss E. helped me cut away some of the leather to give my toes more room. "How... how old are you?"

"Thirteen."

The soldier studies my face again. "I have a girl. Your age," he says. Then he clicks his heels together. I know it's a sign that I'm to get out of his way. I take the bucket— so what if it stinks?—and scurry back to the huts. I can't help feeling a little like a rat.

Jeanette has found the ruler, and Tilly has a piece of wood. All the girls from our hut huddle round as Miss E. shows us how to make a rat trap. Miss E. leans Tilly's piece of wood against the bucket at an angle. "What angle would you say that is?" She asks.

The rest of us laugh when Jeanette raises her hand. She has forgotten that morning lessons are over. "Forty-five degrees," Jeanette says, beaming because she knows the answer.

"Excellent," Miss E. tells her.

Miss E. lays the ruler over the bucket so that the ruler meets the edge of the other strip of wood.

I am starting to understand how the trap will work. A rat will crawl up the angled piece of wood, onto the ruler and then fall into the bucket. But what will we use for bait?

Miss E. has a solution for that too. "I believe I've got an old candy in my apron pocket," she says.

"What *don't* you have in your apron pocket?" Tilly asks. "And if it's a candy, why haven't you eaten it by now— or shared it with us? Have you been hiding it in your pocket since 1942?"

"I'll admit it's practically an antique. But it's licorice flavored, and I've never liked licorice. A rat, however, might feel differently."

Miss E. reaches into her pocket and shows us a candy that is so old and shriveled it looks more like a dried-out bug than a candy. She lays it on the middle of the ruler.

"Now what?" Jeanette asks.

"Do we wait for 'Uncle Edward' to come back?" Cathy asks Miss E.

Miss E. shakes her head. "I'm sure you Girl Guides know the expression *A watched kettle never boils.* Well, here's a variation on a theme. *A watched bucket never catches a rat.* I don't recommend waiting around. Besides, waiting around isn't the Girl Guide way. It's time to do some good turns."

FIVE

Thanks to Miss E., I know a lot about good deeds. For example, I know that some good deeds can be planned ahead of time. Such as remembering a friend's birthday or taking soup to a neighbor who's got a cold. Other good deeds happen on the spot. Like when you see a frail old person in line for broomcorn and let him or her go ahead even when you are ready to collapse from hunger.

When a Girl Guide performs a good deed she must have no expectations of reward. I still have work to do in this department. When I do a good deed I secretly hope Miss E. is watching so she will be impressed. I also like it when the person who is the recipient of my good deed says thank you, but I think that might count as a kind of reward. Then again, it might just be good manners. I agree with Miss E.'s philosophy that good manners matter as much at Weihsien as they do at Buckingham Palace or the White House.

Since I don't have a good deed planned out, I'll have to invent my good deed on the spot. I follow Tilly out of our hut. She needs to use the latrine. I have decided that the first person I meet will be the recipient of my good deed.

Only I don't meet a person. I meet a guard dog. One of the German shepherds that help the Japanese soldiers patrol Weihsien. The dog growls when he sees me. He bares his fangs. They are long, sharp and yellow near the gums.

I stop in my tracks and look around. There is no Japanese soldier nearby. This is the first time I've ever seen a German shepherd alone at Weihsien.

The dog snarls. I take a step back, closer to the hut.

These dogs are trained to kill. It isn't just the gray stone wall with electrified wires running along its top that stops prisoners from trying to escape. It is also the fear of being mauled to death by one of these dogs, who are known for their viciousness. What's strange is that the Japanese soldiers have no fear of the dogs. Just last week I saw a soldier scratching his German shepherd behind its ears, and the dog rolled onto his back and whimpered with pleasure.

"Hello, dog," I say in my friendliest voice. "What are you doing out alone?"

Does speaking kindly to a dog count as a good deed? Maybe not. Especially if the dog doesn't understand English.

The dog comes closer. Am I brave enough to scratch him behind his ears the way I saw the Japanese soldier do? It would probably be smarter to save my good deed for another creature.

That's when I notice the dog is limping. I crouch down, and when I look more closely I see the dog's right front paw is bleeding. A jagged shard of glass is caught at the bottom of his paw. "Come here, boy," I tell him.

The dog must sense I want to help, because he obeys.

My heart beats double time inside my chest. What if he sinks his sharp teeth into me and never lets go? What if he clamps his teeth on my neck and drags me along the road? What if the Japanese soldiers think the dog went after me because I was trying to escape? What if they shoot me before I can explain I was trying to help the dog?

But the dog doesn't bite me or drag me down the road. Instead he drops to his haunches. His snout is so close I can smell his sour dog breath.

I inch my hand toward the wounded paw. I feel his eyes on my fingers. He must be deciding whether or not to attack me.

The dog's blood is bright red. No different than human blood.

I suck in my breath and reach for the wounded paw. Warm dog blood trickles down my hand and over my wrist. There's no time to wipe it away. I reach for the shard of glass, and in one quick move I pull it out from the creature's paw. There is more blood. But now the dog makes a noise I never knew a dog could make—he sighs.

I need to find some way to stop the bleeding. Why didn't I think of that before I removed the shard of glass?

I look around, but I don't see anything that will do the trick.

Then I remember my Girl Guide scarf. I have worn it every day during the time we have been at Weihsien. Miss E. says that wearing our uniforms is good for us because it reminds us who we are and who we want to be. Who I am and who I want to be is a true Girl Guide, someone kind and courageous who thinks of others before herself. Right now the only way to stop this dog from bleeding is to sacrifice my pale-blue scarf.

The cotton is soft and worn from so much wearing, so it's easy to tear a strip off the scarf. The dog watches me, alert, interested. His mouth still hangs open so that I can see his sharp yellow fangs. He is drooling.

"Let me help you," I tell the dog as I reach for his paw again. They say animals can feel fear, and I wonder if this dog knows how afraid I feel right now.

I wrap the strip of pale-blue cotton around the wound as tightly as I can. Because my fingers are trembling, it's hard to get the job done. The dog's blood seeps through the fabric. But once I wrap the paw four times, the bleeding stops. There is just enough loose fabric left for me to tie a knot.

"Good boy," I tell the dog.

If I was braver, I'd scratch behind his ears. But I'm not that brave.

"*Inu!*" an angry-sounding voice calls. *Inu* is the Japanese word for dog. It is the same unsmiling soldier who often inspects our hut in the morning, the one with the small black mustache. The soldier that even Miss E. could not make smile.

The soldier shouts more words in Japanese, but I have no idea what they mean. Is he angry with me—or with the dog?

The dog's ears bend back, and he lunges toward the soldier. That's when the soldier notices the tourniquet. I wonder if he understands I sacrificed my scarf to make it.

I hold out the shard of glass. It still has the dog's blood on it.

I know that the Japanese for "thank you" is *arigatou gozaimasu*. But the Japanese soldier does not say thank you. Instead he blinks, then drops his head and turns his back on me. The dog follows him down the gravel path. He's still limping, but less than before. And though I have to look carefully to see it, the dog's tail is wagging ever so gently.

My heart is still beating double time.

I look at the shard of glass between my fingers and picture the dog's tail wagging gently. That's my reward.

SIX

We've gotten very good at counting in Japanese.

Ichi, ni, san, shi, go, roku, shichi, hachi, kyuu, juu.

Every day at 9:00 AM on the dot and then again at exactly 5:00 PM, the bells ring to announce roll call. Because there are so many prisoners at Weihsien, roll call takes place in different spots around the camp. The 140 children from Chefoo and our teachers meet behind the kitchen down the road from our huts.

It has been pouring rain all afternoon. If only we had umbrellas! Sometimes rain this time of year makes the air in northern China less muggy. But today's rain only makes it muggier.

We form five lines facing the Japanese soldiers and their dogs. We rattle off our numbers in Japanese. The soldiers watch and listen. One records numbers in a small black booklet.

Miss E. thinks roll call is the perfect time to practice good posture. She says that because the spinal column is attached to the brain, keeping our spines straight will help our brains work better. She recommends that we imagine we are hanging from the sky by golden threads attached to the top of our heads. Shoulders back, chins slightly dropped.

Except for our numbers, we are not allowed to say a single word during roll call or to shift in our spots. If we do we could be strapped—or worse! Miss E. says it helps to focus on a spot in the distance. I keep my eyes on the electrified stone wall. It's been getting hotter and more humid every day, and my skin feels clammy underneath my uniform. And this is only May. The next few months will be even worse.

I hear a fly buzzing near my right ear. *Do not land on me*, I tell the fly. I can't say the words out loud. I just hope the fly will read my thoughts. But this fly is not a mind reader, because he lands on the inside of my elbow. If only I could shake him off or swat him with my other hand.

"*Go*," I say. In Japanese, *go* means "five." The Japanese soldier turns his attention to Jeanette, who is sixth in line. The fly takes the tiniest step. I can feel his fly feet moving closer to the bend inside my elbow. I want to scream, but I can't. I pull my shoulders back and try to refocus on the stone wall and the jagged electrified wires that run along the top.

"*Roku*," says Jeanette. She is standing perfectly straight. Even if it isn't very kind, I wish the fly had landed on Jeanette, not me.

I don't dare shake my arm. But then I remember another one of Miss E.'s lessons: there is always a solution if only you can think of it. So without moving even an eighth of an inch, I blow at the fly out of the side of my mouth. I will him to leave my arm. I blow a second time. If Jeanette notices, she cannot say.

The fly takes one more step, then flies off into the rain.

I'm so grateful I could cry, only that would make noise too.

I promise myself that I will not complain during the rest of roll call. I will not complain during any other roll call ever. Girl Guides do not complain. Girl Guides make the best of every situation, even the most challenging ones. The thought makes me stand taller. It makes me want to try to be a better person. The kind of person who doesn't wish a pesky fly had landed on one of her best friends instead of her.

A fat droplet of rain lands just above my lips. I open my mouth and wait to catch it. We get so little fresh water at Weihsien that even a drop of rain is a treat. There, I got it! I savor the taste and the feeling of the droplet trickling down my throat.

I don't realize that Matthew, the rat killer, is standing behind me until he calls out his number. I recognize his voice. I'd like to turn and look at him, but that isn't allowed either. Maybe I will catch a glimpse of him when this roll call finally ends.

I want to smile when I hear Miss E. call out her number. How can she make a Japanese number sound like a song? Though I am staring at the electrified wall and my face shows no emotion, my heart feels strangely full. How lucky we are to have someone like Miss E. looking after us at Weihsien. How would we ever have managed without her?

Now I hear a strange sound, some kind of disturbance coming from the other end of the line, closer to the kitchen. I wish I could turn and see what is going on. The noise gets louder. Even without looking I feel movement at the other end of the line. Not turning to look is even harder than not swatting the fly.

Then Jeanette—Jeanette who never, ever does anything she shouldn't—turns her head.

I turn mine too.

One of the boys has fallen over, probably from hunger or fatigue, or maybe both. What happens next seems to happen in slow motion. As the boy drops to the ground, his foot catches on something I cannot see. I hear a strange sizzling sound. The boy is lying on the earth. His arms are limp by his sides, his face paler than a ghost's.

There is more commotion at the other end of the line. Two of the Japanese soldiers march over to see what has happened. They speak to each other in clipped Japanese. Though I don't understand what they are saying, I know something bad has happened. The third soldier stays in position, his hand on his rifle, eyes flat.

"Oh my god," I hear someone say.

And then I hear someone whisper, "Sagging electrical cable."

I smell burned meat.

At first I think it's food, but then I realize it's the boy. He has been electrocuted.

The Japanese soldiers insist that we finish the roll call. They leave the boy's body on the ground.

When roll call is over, Miss E. stretches out her arms and gathers us together. "Don't look," she whispers, and I know she means we shouldn't look at the corpse. We pass the message along to the other children from Chefoo. "Don't look. Miss E. says not to look."

I don't look.

"*The Lord giveth and the Lord taketh away. Blessed be the name of the Lord,*" Miss E. quotes from the book of Job as she leads us back toward the huts. Her voice is louder than usual.

"*May the name of the Lord be praised,*" several of us say together.

Tilly does not join in the prayer. When I look over at her, I see she is not following Miss E.'s instruction. Tilly is looking at the dead boy. Cathy stops to look at him too. "His boots are in good shape," I hear Cathy say. "Someone had better go back to get those boots."

Miss E.'s body stiffens. "*Ichi, ni, san, shi, go, roku, shichi, hachi, kyuu, juu…*" She sings the Japanese numbers. Loudly.

I join in. So does Jeanette, and all the other girls walking with us.

Miss E. needs us to sing with her. I know because I catch her wiping at her cheek. I don't think the wetness there is only from the rain.

Later I can't stop thinking about how Miss E. raised her voice when she was quoting from the book of Job and singing out numbers in Japanese, and about her wet cheeks. For the first time in the many years that I have known and loved Miss E., I wonder if she is not really as cheerful as she acts.

SEVEN

We are packed together on the sleeping pallet as tightly as sardines in a tin. If I move my elbow even a quarter of an inch, I'll bump into Jeanette. Tilly is on my other side. She isn't worried about disturbing her neighbors. The pallet swarms with lice. When Tilly swats at one she calls out, "Got you!" so loudly that she wakes me from my half sleep.

I turn toward her with a groan.

"I hate it here," she says.

"Shh," I whisper. "Not so loud. You'll wake the others."

"I really hate it here." At least this time she whispers.

"Miss E. says we must do our best," I remind her. "It's hard, but it's the Girl Guide way. Girl Guides do their best, even in the most difficult situations."

Tilly doesn't want to talk about the Girl Guide way. "Did you see the dead boy?" she asks instead. "I heard his name was Daniel. Miss E. will go back for his boots when it's safe to touch him. Another boy will be able to use them. Did you see how his body convulsed before he died? That was from the electrical current."

"Tilly!" I say. "I wish you hadn't told me that." I close my eyes to make the picture in my mind go away. Then I open my eyes again. "Miss E. told us not to look at the corpse."

"You know we don't *always* have to listen to Miss E.," Tilly says. "We're thirteen years old. We can think for ourselves."

Tilly's words feel like a slap. Of course we can think for ourselves. But that doesn't mean we shouldn't listen to Miss E. Instead of trying to explain that to Tilly I look up at the ceiling and wait for sleep to come. If we're lucky, we'll be able to sleep through the night. If we're not so lucky, we'll be awakened by an elbow in our ribs or the noise of a girl getting up to use the honey pot.

But Tilly has more to say. "Miss E. is not our mother."

This time I have an answer. "She is the closest thing we have to a mother," I remind Tilly without taking my eyes off the ceiling. "Our parents deserted us back in Chefoo so they could spread God's word."

Tilly clasps her hands behind her head to make a pillow. "You're right about that." For a few moments neither of us says anything. Then Tilly nudges me in the hip. Because we get so little to eat at Weihsien, I keep getting thinner, and her nudge hurts me more than it would have when we first arrived and my hips had more padding. But I don't cry out because I don't want to awaken Jeanette or any of the other girls on this lice-infested pallet. Just because Tilly doesn't care about the others doesn't mean I have to be like her.

"I'm glad I looked at the dead boy," she says. "At Daniel. And I'm glad some other boy will get his boots."

I let Tilly have the last word. Otherwise I won't get any sleep. Then how will I be able to do my chores and do good deeds tomorrow?

In my time at Weihsien I have learned that memory is complicated. Before I came here I didn't know that a happy memory could hurt more than a nudge to the hip. That is why I try *not* to remember the days when I still lived with my parents, before they left me at the boarding school in Chefoo. It's as if I keep those memories in a special box (I don't know why, but in my imagination the box is long and thin and made of cardboard) and hardly ever take the box out of my head.

Sometimes, though, memories come out of nowhere, the way I remembered my mother when Miss E. was giving us the crushed-eggshell paste.

When I feel very brave or when, for some reason, I feel a need to open that box of memories, I let myself do it.

That's what I do now as I try to fall back asleep. I take out the box and open it just a crack. I let myself think of my mother—without the usual anger I feel when I remember her. I think of how her head tilts to one side when she laughs, how her blue eyes sparkle when she talks about the Lord and how she used to squeeze my hand when we took a walk or sat side by side in church. I think of how my mother smells like lavender. She kept a bottle of lavender water on the bureau in her room and dabbed some on her wrists every morning. Sometimes she dabbed a little on my wrists too. "Don't tell your father," she'd say, winking at me.

Is my mind playing tricks on me? Because though I know I'm in our hut at Weihsien, I smell lavender—flowery, sweet and clean. It's the most delicious thing I ever smelled.

Maybe I dreamed of lavender fields.

It's not the delicious fragrance of lavender that wakes me up. It's the sharp stench of fresh urine. One of the other girls has used the honey pot.

Next to me, Jeanette trembles in her sleep. My body stiffens when I remember what Tilly told me about how Daniel convulsed before he died. Has Jeanette been electrocuted? No, I tell myself, that's impossible. There's no sagging electrical cable in the hut, and Jeanette hasn't been standing out in the rain, making her even more likely to be electrocuted.

I run my fingers across Jeanette's forehead. "Everything's okay," I whisper.

The trembling stops, and Jeanette opens her eyes. She looks relieved to see me. That's when I know she was in the middle of a nightmare.

"I saw him," she says.

I don't have to ask her who she saw.

Daniel.

"He was lying on the ground, dead, and we were walking right over him. All of us. As if he wasn't even there. We could hear his bones crunching under our feet." Jeanette's voice breaks.

"Everything's okay," I whisper again. "It was just a dream."

Tilly wakes up and turns onto her side. She rolls her eyes when she hears what I tell Jeanette. "Don't you see, Gwen," Tilly mutters, "that everything is *not* okay?"

Jeanette sniffles. So does Cathy, who has overheard our conversation.

I glare at Tilly. How can she be so heartless?

EIGHT

We usually have a lesson after our morning routine—prayers, broomcorn, sweeping out the hut and roll call—but today Miss E. thinks we should try changing our routine.

"But aren't you the one who's always saying routine is good for us?" Tilly asks Miss E.

"I do say that," Miss E. admits. "But we can't let ourselves be enslaved to anything—including routine."

"We're enslaved to the Japs," Tilly says. "And there isn't much we can do about that!"

"Matilda! Watch your language!" Miss E.'s voice is firm, not angry. "We're not slaves. We're *sojourners*. And by the way, I'd prefer if you used the term *Japanese* instead of *Japs*. It's more polite."

Jeanette raises her hand. "If we're changing our routine, what will we do instead of lessons?" she asks.

"Rat catching!" Miss E. sings out the answer. She makes rat catching sound like we are going to see a movie or to the world's fair. "I've decided today will be the official contest. The children from all the other huts will be participating too. That makes 140 rat catchers in all."

"You said there'd be a prize," Jeanette reminds her.

Dot, whose expression is almost always sad or grumpy, brightens at the mention of a prize.

Miss E. claps. "Of course there will be a prize. I'm just not at liberty to tell you what that prize will be."

"Is it food?" Tilly asks. Like me, Tilly scraped her frying pan clean this morning. Our pans and plates are getting scratched from all our scraping. When your stomach is empty, it's hard to think of anything else.

"Maybe yes—maybe no," Miss E. says. "You don't want to eat rat fricassee, do you?"

We've never heard the word *fricassee* before. Just the sound of it makes us laugh. *Fricassee!*

Miss E. sends Cathy to check on our rat trap. Cathy calls back that the piece of wood on the side of the bucket has fallen over—and the candy is missing. Miss E. rubs her hands together. "How exciting!" she says.

Miss E. finds a second candy in her apron pocket. This one looks even older and more shriveled than the first. "A little music might also help us catch rats."

"I had no idea rats were musical," Jeanette says.

"They like the flute. Or at least they did in the town

of Hamelin, when the Pied Piper paid a visit," Miss E. explains. "Girl Guides, do you know that story?"

"Of course we know the story of the Pied Piper. It's famous," Dot tells Miss E. "But we don't have a flute." She shakes her head sadly when she says this.

Miss E. grins. "What you mean to say is that we don't have a flute *yet*."

Jeanette tugs on Miss E.'s apron. "Did you bring a flute from Chefoo? And if you did, why didn't you let us try it?"

"I never said I brought a flute from Chefoo. In fact, I didn't. But I'm about to show you girls how to *make* a flute."

"A person can't just *make* a flute," Tilly says flatly.

Miss E. makes a tut-tut sound. "Matilda, Matilda. I wish you wouldn't use the word *can't* so often. It lacks possibility."

Miss E. reaches into her trunk of school supplies and takes out a sheet of fine vellum drawing paper. She waves the sheet in the air like the white flag the teachers hung out at our school in Chefoo to tell the Japanese we had surrendered.

Has Miss E. had that vellum in her trunk of school supplies since we left Chefoo? And if so, why haven't I ever seen it before? I can't help imagining how lovely it would feel to draw on such a fancy sheet of paper. Miss E. rolls the sheet into a tight cylinder, then holds it in place by fastening a rubber band at either end.

"Let me try," Tilly says, taking the rolled-up vellum from Miss E. and blowing into it. All we hear is Tilly's breath— and it doesn't sound very musical.

Cathy grabs the vellum from Tilly and blows into it. The sound is just as bad.

"Not so fast! I wasn't finished!" Miss E. retrieves the cylinder. "If there was a badge for patience, I don't think you two Girl Guides would get it." We watch as Miss E. finds a splinter of wood from the pallet and uses it to dig a hole into the paper at one end.

"Um," Jeanette says, "I don't mean to seem impatient, but is it ready now? And if it is, can I try it next? I've always wanted to play the flute."

"Just let me poke a few more holes," Miss E. tells her. The first hole Miss E. poked went through all the layers of paper. The next ones only pierce two layers. "All righty then, Jeanette, since you've always wanted to play the flute, you can be the first to test this one out."

I've never seen Jeanette look so happy. For a moment I remember how upset she was after her bad dream last night, and I feel so grateful to Miss E. for finding a way to cheer her up.

Jeanette blows into the paper flute. What comes out isn't exactly music, but it isn't exactly breath either. It's something in between.

All the girls in the hut clap. I clap loudest of all.

Tilly crosses her arms over her chest. "I don't think you have a talent for playing the flute," she tells Jeanette.

"Talent isn't something that a person *has*," Miss E. says. "It's something that a person *cultivates*. A little like a garden.

If Jeanette decides to cultivate her musical talent, I'm sure she will succeed. Even on a paper flute."

Which is how Jeanette ends up kneeling by the bucket, playing Miss E.'s homemade paper flute. The sound isn't exactly pleasant, but then again, cultivating talent—like cultivating a garden—must take time.

Tilly lays the second old candy on the middle of the ruler placed across the top of the bucket.

Our first rat visitor turns up about fifteen minutes later. Miss E. tells us with her eyes to stay calm and not to move a muscle. Jeanette closes her eyes as she blows into the paper flute. Maybe the Pied Piper was onto something—maybe rats really do like music.

The rat's whiskers twitch—I think he smells licorice. We watch, spellbound, as he scurries up the first piece of wood, crosses the ruler and reaches for the candy. Then *plop* he goes, right into the bottom of the bucket.

We clap even louder than we did for Jeanette's performance.

"Now what?" Eunice asks Miss E.

"Now we wait for the rest of his family to come and check on this fellow's whereabouts," Miss E. says.

We can hear the rat scrabbling in the bottom of the bucket. He doesn't sound very glad to be there.

Jeanette puts down her flute. I expect her to be happy, but instead she looks sad. Is she remembering the boy from her dream? But that isn't what's bothering her. "It isn't right to keep the rat a prisoner," Jeanette says.

"It's better than clubbing him to death," Tilly tells her.

"It isn't right to keep anyone a prisoner." Jeanette seems to be talking to herself.

Miss E. pats Jeanette's hand. "Once the contest is over, I'm going to ask one of the coolies to release the rats we've caught and let them free outside the gates. So the rats won't be our prisoners."

The coolies are the local Chinese workers who empty our honey pots outside the walls of Weihsien and do other chores for the Japanese army. Jeanette's face relaxes when she hears Miss E.'s plan.

As usual, Tilly wants to get in the last word. "If only," she mutters, "the Japs—I should say, the Japanese— didn't insist on making prisoners—excuse me, I mean *sojourners*—out of *us*."

NINE

Leave it to Miss E. to turn rat catching into a lesson.

Tilly says she's not in the mood for more lessons having to do with rat catching. "Didn't we already learn plenty about engineering by building the trap?" she asks Miss E. "We could build a bridge with what you've taught us!"

Miss E. smiles indulgently. "There is quite a difference between building a rat trap and a bridge. Besides, I was thinking of something a little more artistic for today's lesson."

"Are we going to draw?" I ask hopefully. What I really want to know is whether Miss E. has any more vellum paper in her supply trunk.

"No drawing just now," Miss E. says. "I think it's time for something literary. Which is why I've decided to teach you Girl Guides how to write haiku."

"Aren't haiku Japanese poems?" Cathy asks. "If the Japanese are our enemies, why would you want us to study their poetry?"

"Hmm," Miss E. says. I can tell from her *Hmm* that she is thinking of the best way to answer Cathy's question. "Let's say I prefer not to think of the Japanese as our enemies. It's true that we've met some Japanese soldiers who can be, well…rather harsh, but it would be poor logic to conclude that every single Japanese person is like that. Besides, if we're *sojourners* here, then the Japanese are our *hosts*. Even when we don't see eye to eye, we can always learn from our hosts. Especially hosts with such a rich and ancient culture."

Tilly nods in agreement. "As you know, I'm no fan of the Japs—I should say, the Japanese—but I do like haiku. And I'm very good at writing them."

Miss E. claps her hands. "What wonderful news, Matilda! Why then, why don't I rest my vocal cords while you explain to all the other girls what a haiku is and how it works?" She waves her hand in the air in front of her. "Take it away, Matilda. I know you'll do an outstanding job. You're a smart girl, and you're good at explaining things."

I am so used to Tilly arguing that I am a little surprised when she turns to the rest of us and actually starts explaining what haiku is. I've heard of it too, but I'd never say so. Still, Tilly does seem to know a lot about the subject.

"Haiku is the most popular form of Japanese poetry," she begins. "A haiku consists of seventeen syllables—

five in the first line, seven in the second and five in the last. And the poems never rhyme."

Jeanette sighs. "If that's true, I don't think I'll like them very much. Because I love poetry that rhymes. I'd hardly call it poetry if it doesn't rhyme."

Tilly gives Jeanette a sharp look. "Haiku does not rhyme. And it is definitely poetry. My father loves haiku." Tilly's parents are also missionaries. This is the first time she's said anything about her father's interest in poetry.

"Have you heard of Matsuo Bashō?" Miss E. asks. I think she is trying to prevent an argument between the two girls. Tilly and Jeanette are like oil and water— two substances that do not mix together well. But I get along with both of them. Maybe it's because there's oil and also water in me.

We shake our heads. We've never heard of Matsuo Bashō.

But Tilly says she has. "Of course I've heard of him. Who hasn't?" It's obvious she enjoys acting as if she knows more than we do. "He was an important Japanese poet during the sixteenth century."

"Seventeenth," Miss E. corrects her.

"That's what I said…seventeenth," Tilly says.

Jeanette raises her hand. "You said sixteenth." Jeanette turns to me. "Didn't she say sixteenth?"

I hate being caught in the middle of oil and water. But Tilly did say sixteenth. I am about to say so when Miss E.

intervenes again. "Matsuo Bashō was an important practitioner of haiku. Did you know," she asks Tilly, "that he came from a family of warriors?"

"Of course I knew that," Tilly says, but when she looks away from Miss E., I'm not so sure she's telling the truth. "Matsuo Bashō was a warrior until he began writing haiku. Then he became a poet instead of a warrior."

"Exactly," Miss E. says. She turns to look at all of us as if Tilly has said something very important that she wants us to think about. Miss E. probably thinks the world would be a better place if the entire Imperial Japanese Amy laid down their rifles and bayonets and started writing haiku instead.

She tells us that her favorite haiku was written by Matsuo Bashō—and she asks whether we want her to recite it to us. Of course the answer is yes. "Please!" some of the girls squeal.

Miss E. crosses her hands in front of her, just below her hips. Her eyes get a dreamy look as she recites the poem.

Won't you come and see
loneliness? Only one leaf
from the kiri tree.

"Is that it?" Dot sounds disappointed.

"I think I'd like it more if it rhymed," Jeanette adds.

Tilly is counting out syllables on her fingers. "Yes," she says, "that's seventeen in all. Five in the first line—"

"What is a kiri tree?" Cathy interrupts. "I don't think I ever saw one."

Miss E. uncrosses her hands. "*Kiri* is the Japanese word. We call them *Paulownia*. They have beautiful heart-shaped leaves."

It's hard for me to follow so many different conversations. That's because, even if they do not rhyme, those simple seventeen syllables have affected me. Though I am surrounded by my friends and Miss E., I am suddenly so lonely that the feeling makes my body ache.

I also wish that I could make a drawing. If I could, I know exactly what I'd draw: a single heart-shaped leaf.

But Miss E. wants us to try writing our own haiku.

We take out our notebooks.

Tilly is already scribbling away. She fills a page with haiku in no time. I think she has inherited her father's love of poetry.

Jeanette raises her hand again. "Miss E., I have an important question. Are we supposed to write about something beautiful—like the kiri tree?"

"Most haiku are about beautiful things," Miss E. tells her. "But the main goal is to get the syllables right—and also to express what's in your heart. Even if it isn't beautiful."

I think about scribbling whatever's in my mind—the way Tilly is doing. (She's already started another page in her notebook.) But I don't think that approach to haiku writing suits me. Instead I close my eyes and give the words and ideas time to brew.

I hope Miss E. will not mind that I've decided to write a haiku about the dead rat Matthew brought to show us.

He has a dead rat
In his arms the dead rat lies
Do rats have souls too?

Miss E. could look over our shoulders to see what we are writing, but she doesn't. I think she wants us to have some privacy. Wherever we go in Weihsien, we're always crowded together. Though we girls are sitting close to each other, writing a haiku makes me feel as if I have some space.

I count the syllables in my haiku. Exactly seventeen. Maybe one day I'll write a haiku about Daniel, the boy who was electrocuted.

TEN

The boys from Matthew's hut win the rat-catching contest. They catch—and kill—six rats. There are only two rats rattling around in our bucket.

There are boys in his hut who are taller and stronger than Matthew is. One boy named Benton is nearly six feet tall. Another, named Amos, has the broadest shoulders I've ever seen. While most of the boys who help with pumping water from the wells need to rest after a one-hour shift, a boy named Tyler can work for two hours straight. But Matthew is the spokesperson for the boys in his hut. Even if he is a rat killer, there is something I like about him. It isn't his looks, though he isn't ugly. I think it's that there is something smart and a bit mischievous about him. Something playful.

"We're here for our prize," Matthew tells Miss E. All the boys from his hut are standing at the door behind him.

We've all been wondering what the prize will be. Maybe a chocolate bar that Miss E. has been hoarding. Or a tin of sugar cookies. And if it isn't food—though we're all hoping it's something to eat—maybe it's a board for playing checkers or a book the boys can read aloud. If it is a book, once they've finished reading it, we can borrow it. That's exactly the kind of prize Miss E. would come up with.

"A little music, please," Miss E. says, looking over at Jeanette, who takes out the paper flute and plays a victory tune.

Miss E. is hiding the prize behind her back. I know that we girls are all thinking the same thing: if only our rat trap had been more effective. Then the chocolate bar would be ours. Though I have not had chocolate in nearly two and a half years, I can practically taste how delicious it is.

When Miss E. brings her hands from behind her back and presents the prize to Matthew, we are all disappointed. It's a small, dented can of evaporated milk with the label coming loose. What kind of prize is that?

"I found it last week at the bottom of my trunk," Miss E. explains. "It doesn't look very nice, but each of you boys on the winning team can have a sip. It doesn't taste as good as fresh milk, but I think you'll still enjoy it."

"Why, uh, thank you," Matthew says. The fact that he is trying to be gracious makes me like him even more.

"It's the best I could do under the circumstances," Miss E. says. "But you can always try imagining that it is something better. In the world of imagination, nothing is impossible."

"I was hoping it would be something to eat. A person can't eat evaporated milk," a boy whose name I don't know calls out.

"I was hoping for a trophy," Benton adds.

Miss E. clears her throat. "There is another prize—for all of you. Not only the boys," she adds. "It's a very special prize."

We have made several circles around Miss E., and now we make our circles tighter as we move closer in.

"I know you're expecting a thing," Miss E. says. "An object of some kind. Like a book or a trophy or some food that is more delicious than boring old evaporated milk. But this prize I have for all of you isn't a thing." She pauses to build suspense. "It's a person."

A person? How can a person be a prize?

We all look around, but we don't see anyone who could be the prize Miss E. is talking about.

"Mr. Liddell?" Miss E. sings out.

A tall lanky man pops out from behind our hut. Has he been hiding there all this time?

"I'd like all of you to meet Mr. Lid—"

"It's Eric Liddell!" I hear Matthew tell the other boys. "The man people call Jesus in Running Shoes. I recognize him from the newspaper clippings. I heard he was at Weihsien, but I never saw him before."

Mr. Liddell takes a small bow. "I'm delighted to meet you, boys and girls," he says. He speaks with a thick Scottish accent. "Eliza—excuse me, I should say, Miss E.—asked me whether I might give you youngsters some pointers about running, and of course I agreed. It isn't easy to say no to a person as determined as Eliza—er, Miss E."

This is the first time I have heard Miss E. called anything except Miss E. The name Eliza comes as a bit of a shock to me. But then, I think, why should it? It isn't as if her parents took one look at her and named her Miss E.

"P-pointers about running from Er-Eric Liddell?" Matthew can hardly get the words out. "He won a gold medal in the four-hundred-meter run at the 1924 Olympics. We're thrilled to finally meet you, sir." Matthew reaches out to shake Eric Liddell's hand but then forgets to let it go.

Jeanette raises her hand. "Why did you call him Jesus in Running Shoes?" she asks Matthew.

Mr. Liddell raises his palm in the air to signal that he wants to stop the conversation. "You're embarrassing me," he says. "I won't deny that back in 1924 I took part in the Paris Olympics..."

Matthew tells the rest of the story. "Mr. Liddell didn't just take part in the Paris Olympics. He trained for the hundred-meter race. But when he found out that the qualifying heats would be on a Sunday—the Lord's Day— he withdrew."

Miss E. smiles approvingly at Mr. Liddell.

Matthew has more to say. "When Mr. Liddell competed in the four-hundred-meter race instead, no one expected him to even place. People said he hadn't trained for the four-hundred-meter. But he won the gold medal—and set a world record."

Everyone claps. Mr. Liddell blushes. Miss E. looks on as proudly as if she had won the gold medal herself. "Well, well," Mr. Liddell says, "I would never have won that race without the Good Lord's help. At any rate, that's enough about me. I think it's time we move on to some pointers to help you with your own running. Maybe one of you will go on to win gold one day."

Tilly sighs. "It's an honor to meet you, sir, but the truth is, there's no room for us to run anywhere at Weihsien. There isn't room to do a jumping jack." When Tilly stretches out her arms, she bumps into me on one side and Benton on the other.

"That fact occurred to me and to El—I should say, Miss E.," Mr. Liddell tells Tilly. "But there is always a solution—if only you can think of it." That's exactly the kind of thing Miss E. would say. No wonder she and Mr. Liddell are friends.

"For example," Mr. Liddell continues, "not many people know about the importance of foot-strengthening exercises. Most people ignore their feet altogether, though our feet work harder than any other part of our bodies."

Jeanette raises her hand again. I wish she'd stop doing that. "What about our brains? Don't our brains work harder than our feet?" she asks.

"Point well taken," Mr. Liddell says. "Our brains probably work just as hard as our feet. You obviously possess a hard-working brain, young lady."

Jeanette's face lights up. "Thank you, sir."

"So if you young people are willing, and since I agreed to be your prize for your excellent participation in Weihsien's very first rat-catching competition, I thought I'd start by teaching you some basic foot exercises. If you could each raise your right foot—an inch or two off the ground will do. Yes, that's perfect. Let it hover. Now rotate your foot slightly to the right. Three rotations. Excellent. Try not to bump into your neighbor. Now to the left…"

Miss E. does the exercises too.

Mr. Liddell wants us to flex our feet, then point them. "Miss E.," he says, "you're doing beautifully. Of course, that's no surprise considering you were a ballerina."

Now it's Miss E.'s turn to blush.

My left foot, which was raised in the air, falls to the ground.

Miss E. a ballerina?

I never would have guessed it.

ELEVEN

I'm glad I'm not a grown-up.

Grown-ups are too, well, grown-up. They never get to play. Of course there are exceptions like Miss E. She's the most playful grown-up I know. It's one of the reasons we all love her so much. Some grown-ups forget what it means to be a child, but not Miss E.

At Weihsien the grown-ups work extremely hard. Besides looking after us and giving us lessons, Miss E. works in the camp kitchen and sometimes in the infirmary. That's why her hands are always red and the skin on her fingertips is cracking. From so much scrubbing and looking after ill people. The infirmary has fifty rusty iron cots that are always in use. Aside from dysentery, a highly contagious stomach infection, other common illnesses here at Weihsien include beriberi, which comes from having a poor diet; hepatitis B, which attacks the liver; typhus, which comes from drinking dirty water; and jaundice, which makes the whites of your eyes turn yellow. And, of course, many of the people who end up in the infirmary are there because they are dehydrated and malnourished, making them too weak to work and sometimes even too weak to stand. It's a wonder we aren't all in the infirmary, really.

Even Mr. Liddell, an Olympic gold-medal winner, has to report for work detail. The other day I saw him chopping wood, his forehead and arms as sweaty as they must have been when he ran the four-hundred-meter dash. I wonder if, while he chops, he ever remembers what it felt like to win gold. Or if, like me, Mr. Liddell finds some happy memories too painful to remember.

We have to work too. Only the very youngest children at Weihsien are exempt from work detail. Most of those children live with their parents in the few huts reserved for families, on the western side of the camp, across from the ladies' dormitory.

The boys from Chefoo work mostly at the wells, pumping water, which they then have to boil and distill. Most of the other girls from our boarding school work in the eggplant field or in one of the kitchens. Dot works in the guardhouse, cleaning and preparing green tea for the Japanese soldiers in the afternoon.

Jeanette has the best job. She rings the bells for roll call. But Jeanette says bell ringing is harder than it sounds, that pulling on the ropes to activate the bells hurts her neck and shoulders. She also has to rush like crazy to be on time for roll call herself. The one time she was late, she got two smacks across the face. And when she cried, she got two more.

The fear of being shouted at or smacked makes all of us work very hard.

Tilly and I are assigned to clean the mess hall where we get our meals—if you can use the word *meals* to describe the scraps they feed us. Tilly and I always begin by sweeping the floor, collecting dirt in an oversized tin dustpan.

This afternoon Tilly must be checking for crumbs too. That's what happens when you're starving. Back in Chefoo I'd never have eaten anything from the floor, but here I always hope to find a crumb or two. Today there is only grit and sand in our sweepings. I shouldn't be surprised. Who would be foolish enough to let a single crumb fall to the floor of the mess hall?

I want to ask Tilly if she was as surprised as me to learn that Miss E. was once a ballerina named Eliza. But a Japanese soldier is supervising us, and chatting is forbidden during work detail.

This soldier grunts orders. When he sees that the dustpan is getting full, he lifts his chin toward the door and double-grunts. That means it's time for me to empty the dustpan outside. As I get up from the floor, I am careful not to let any of the grit fall out. I have seen other children punished for far less serious offenses. Usually the punishment is two slaps across the face, like the ones Jeanette got, or a swift hard kick in the legs or belly.

Once I saw a Japanese soldier twist a child's arm like it was a dishrag he was wringing out.

I go to empty the dustpan at the side of the mess hall, close to where the nearest kitchen is.

As I am about to turn the corner, I spot Miss E. My heart leaps. She is carrying a basket filled with eggplants so purple they're almost black. Eggplant is the only vegetable we get at Weihsien. "Miss—" I start to call out, but then I stop myself. What if the guard has followed me outside? I don't want him to twist my arm or kick me.

Miss E. does not notice me. Now I see why—Mr. Liddell is with her. I didn't see him before because he was hidden behind the eggplants.

"I'm terribly worried," I hear Miss E. tell him.

They put down their baskets, and I wonder if it is a coincidence that they have met up here or whether they planned it.

I know I should announce that I am nearby or leave. It isn't right to listen in on other people's conversations. But something makes me stay where I am, frozen in my spot. Miss E. is usually so cheerful and optimistic. The only time I ever saw her get upset was after Daniel's death. So why in the world would a person like Miss E. feel worried? I can almost feel the ground shift underneath me.

A small, hard lump begins to form at the bottom of my throat. If Miss E. is worried—no, *terribly* worried—then something must have gone awfully, *terribly* wrong.

"You mustn't worry, Eliza," I hear Mr. Liddell say. He reaches for Miss E.'s hand, but then he lets his arm drop to his side. "Worrying," I hear him tell her, "is like praying for bad things to happen."

I can see from the creases on Miss E.'s forehead that she is thinking about Mr. Liddell's words. I am thinking about them too. Mr. Liddell thinks worrying can make things worse. Is that possible? If Miss E. is right that being cheerful and doing good deeds makes life better, then doesn't it make sense that being sour and worrying can make things worse?

"Everything is in the Good Lord's hands," Mr. Liddell assures Miss E.

Miss E. shakes her head. "What about the Nanking Massacre?" she asks Mr. Liddell. "Are you saying that was in the Good Lord's hands too?" And now Miss E. makes a sound I've never ever heard her make before. She whimpers. At first I can hardly believe my ears. Miss E. whimpering? When she does it again, I know I've heard right. The sound reminds me of the German shepherd with the piece of glass in his paw.

Mr. Liddell wraps his arms around Miss E., but she shakes them loose.

"Hundreds of thousands of innocent people were murdered by Japanese troops in Nanking. Hundreds of thousands." Miss E.'s shoulders tremble as she speaks. And there's the whimper again. "And worse."

What could be worse than the murder of hundreds of thousands of innocent people?

I try to remember everything I ever heard about Nanking. In one of our geography lessons we learned that Nanking is the capital of the Republic of China. But Miss E. never said anything about a massacre.

I cannot help shivering when I suddenly remember how once or twice I heard my parents mention the capital city. When they said *Nanking* they always dropped their voices. Was that because they didn't want me knowing about the massacre?

"You know what upsets me most of all?" Miss E. asks Mr. Liddell. "That try as I might, I may not be able to protect my children."

I haven't moved from my spot. When Miss E. says *my children*, I know she means us. Those two words feel like a warm bath or a good meal eaten in front of the fire. For a moment I even forget how hungry I am. Miss E. thinks of us—of me—as if she was our mother.

I expect Mr. Liddell to start talking about the Good Lord again. But what he says next has nothing to do with religion. "You may not be able to protect them."

Not be able to protect us?

What does that mean?

I cover my mouth so Miss E. and Mr. Liddell won't hear me gasp. The water in my imaginary bath turns cold, and I remember how hungry I am.

TWELVE

I need to learn more about the Nanking Massacre, but I don't know where to go or who to ask. If I ask Miss E., she'll know I was listening in. Besides, Miss E. doesn't like to discuss upsetting subjects. But I don't want to live in a bubble. And a part of me is starting to think that is what Miss E. has been trying to do—keep us in a kind of bubble. What if I want answers—even if the answers are upsetting?

Some of the teachers from Chefoo have set up a small lending library in one of the huts. So after the Japanese soldier grunts to indicate that our work in the mess hall is finished, I tell Tilly I'm going to see if there's anything new at the library.

Of course, new means new to me. All the books in the lending library are old, with pages that are yellow and worn.

The lending library is really just two lopsided wooden crates. A boy is already there, hunched over the crates. Because I don't want to startle him, I announce myself by saying, "I hope you remembered your library card."

The boy answers with a deep laugh. When he turns to look at me, I am surprised to see it's Matthew.

"It's you," I can't help blurting out. "The rat killer."

"No one ever called me that before," Matthew says, "but I guess it fits. What's your name?"

"Gwen."

"Gwen."

I never really thought about my own name before. For me, it's just something I always had, like my dirty-blond hair or my ten toes. But something about the way Matthew says it makes me realize for the first time that I like my own name.

"What book did you find?" I ask Matthew.

He holds the book out so I can see its cover. "*Around the World in Eighty Days*. It's an adventure story by Jules Verne. I always wanted to read it."

"It sounds good," I say. "Now if you could move over, I'd like to look for a book too."

Matthew takes two steps away from the crates. "You won't find much. It's mostly just schoolbooks and religious tracts. What kind of book were you hoping for?"

"A book about Chinese history. I want to learn about the Nanking Massacre." I don't know why I'm telling the rat killer all this.

Matthew looks at me like he is seeing me for the first time. "Aren't you a little young to read about massacres?"

I throw my shoulders back so that I'll look taller—and older. "I'm thirteen."

"That old?"

I can't tell if Matthew is teasing. "How old are you?" I ask him.

"Fifteen," he says. "Old enough to know all about the Nanking Massacre."

"I heard that hundreds of thousands of innocent Chinese were killed." I pause before I add, "And worse." I watch Matthew's face for his reaction.

"The Imperial Japanese Army can be very cruel," is all he says. "But I don't think you'll find any books about the Nanking Massacre here in Weihsien. The Japs would never allow it."

"Would you ever like to go around the world in eighty days?" I ask Matthew.

"Who wouldn't?"

"Does that mean yes?"

"Of course it means yes. I would like to go around the world in eighty days. If we get out of here alive." He practically spits out the words.

"We'll get out of here alive," I tell him.

"You don't know that for sure," Matthew says.

"I do know it. For sure." As soon as the words are out of my mouth, I realize how young and foolish I must sound.

Because I don't know what else to say, I add, "Miss E. is sure we'll get out alive. I trust Miss E."

"Miss E. and Mr. Liddell are believers," Matthew says. "That's why they don't have doubts. You must be a believer too." I can tell from the way he says it that Matthew doesn't have a high opinion of believers.

"Are you saying you aren't a believer?" I ask. "Aren't your parents missionaries too?"

"Even if my parents *were* missionaries," Matthew says, "which they aren't, I wouldn't *have* to be a believer. A person doesn't always have to agree with his parents— or his teachers."

"I thought all the children from Chefoo had parents who were missionaries," I say.

"In that case, I'm an exception. My father is a tea importer. He travels around China doing business. I wanted to go with him, but he left me at Chefoo so I could keep studying. He meant well. The Chefoo School was known for its high standards. But then look what happened." Matthew lifts his eyes toward the dirty, cracked window and the watchtower outside.

"At least we've been able to keep up with our school-work," I say. "Thanks to Miss E. and the other teachers."

"It isn't the same as being at a real school."

"Of course it isn't. But it's still something. And I'm grateful for it." I wonder if Matthew knows what I'm thinking— that he could try being a little more grateful himself.

"What about your mother?" I ask. "You didn't mention her. Only your father the tea importer."

"My mother died when I was little. I don't remember her."

"I'm sorry."

Matthew presses the book he's borrowed to his chest—like a shield. "A person can't miss what he never had," he says. "I should let you find a book, Gwen."

I reach out to touch Matthew's elbow, but then I stop myself. "Before you go, can you tell me any more about the massacre? I overheard Miss E. talking about it with Mr. Liddell. She was upset. Which is unusual for Miss E. She's always so cheerful."

I can feel Matthew's eyes on me, deciding how much to say. "You've seen how brutal the Japanese soldiers can be," he says. "Let's just say they were even more brutal in Nanking."

"What do you mean by *even more brutal*?"

"Here's an example for you. During the Nanking Massacre, two Japanese officers had a killing contest."

"A killing contest? You mean like our rat-killing contest?"

"Something like that—only worse. The two officers wanted to see who could be the first to kill one hundred people, using only a sword. They didn't only kill Chinese soldiers. They killed innocent civilians." Matthew pauses. When he speaks, his voice is not much louder than a whisper. "Including women and girls." He lets those last four words sink in and then he adds, "We need to get out of here, Gwen."

"We'll get out when the war is over," I tell him. "Miss E. says it will be soon. Until then we have to make the best of a difficult situation. It's one of the Girl Guide laws."

I don't expect Matthew to agree.

But I also don't expect him to react the way he does.

He laughs.

THIRTEEN

There is always a long lineup outside the latrine.

An old man with bony, hunched shoulders stands off to the side, away from the others. As I get closer I see the dark dribbles along one of his scrawny legs. He must have lost control of his bowels. Terrible diarrhea is a sign of dysentery. The others keep away because of the stench and because they are afraid to catch the disease.

Only one woman is brave enough to approach the man. I can only see the back of her. She hands the man a scrap of fabric, or maybe it's a leaf she found on the ground. We use leaves for toilet paper at Weihsien. Then the woman pats the man's back. I think it's her way of telling him not to feel ashamed.

When the woman turns around, I realize it's Miss E. My cheeks get hot. I've never seen her in line here before. I know it's normal to empty our bladders and bowels, but I still don't like to imagine the teacher I so respect squatted over one of the stinking toilets.

Miss E. does not seem embarrassed to see me. "Why, hello, Gwen," she says cheerfully.

"Good afternoon, Miss E." I can't look her in the eye. If I do, I'll picture her squatted over a filthy toilet.

"*Teng chu!*" a voice calls out. It's one of the coolies. He's carrying a honey pot, and he wants us to make room so he can pass. We all move to the left—away from the old man. We don't want to be splashed with what's inside a honey pot.

I've never spoken to a coolie. I've never even looked one in the eye. Though they're not prisoners, people say their lives aren't much better than ours. I can't think of a worse job than lugging honey pots and emptying them into some cesspool outside the camp.

As the coolie passes, Miss E. reaches out to pat his elbow and whispers, "*Xiexie,*" which is Chinese for *thank you*.

The coolie is so startled that he loses his footing. The honey pot lurches to one side. Without thinking, I reach out to catch it. But in the end the coolie doesn't need my help. He regains his balance and his grip on the honey pot. Unfortunately, a little of the stinking *honey* lands on my forearm. I know not to wipe it away with my fingers. Instead I bend down and rub my forearm in the dirt. What I'd do for a hot bath and a real bar of soap!

Later, when we are back in the hut, someone knocks at the window. I'm closest, so Miss E. asks me to check and see who it is. I hope it's Matthew. But it isn't. It's the coolie from this afternoon. "It's your friend," I tell Miss E.

"Do you mean Mr. Liddell?" she asks.

"No, your friend from the latrine. The coolie."

When Miss E. opens the door, she looks both ways to make sure no one is watching. Coolies aren't supposed to be visiting us.

"What have you got there?" Miss E. asks with a giggle. "Oh my! What a little sweetheart!"

The rest of us gather around to see what is making Miss E. giggle.

When I hear a squeal, I think at first that it's Jeanette, who has a high-pitched laugh. I elbow my way through the crowd of girls to get a better view of what the coolie has brought Miss E.

It's the world's tiniest piglet. He has beady yellowish-brown eyes, a pale pink snout and the sweetest curly tail.

Tilly puts her hands on her hips. "Is he for eating?" she asks.

Miss E. is cradling the piglet in her arms. "I certainly hope not, Matilda," she says. "Don't you think he'd make a nice pet?" Then she turns back to the coolie. "*Xiexie,*" she tells him, putting her hand over her heart.

The coolie doesn't speak English. But he points to his own chest and says, "*Lu.*" That must be his name.

"I'm Miss E.," Miss E. says. "*Xiexie,* Lu."

Miss E. can only string together a few phrases in Chinese, and Lu doesn't speak any English. But that doesn't stop them from having a conversation with hand gestures instead of words.

Miss E. has a question. With the piglet still in her arms, she gestures for Lu to follow her. She brings him to the back of the hut where we've been keeping the bucket with the two rats inside. Lu peers into the bucket, then looks back at Miss E. as if he is awaiting instructions. "Can you get rid of them?" she asks. Lu shakes his head and shrugs. He doesn't know what she wants. When Miss E. waves her hands away from her, Lu nods excitedly. He understands that Miss E. wants him to get rid of the rats.

Jeanette goes to her trunk and comes back with a pink baby bonnet, which she ties on the little piglet's head. We all laugh at the sight—even Lu, who slaps his leg, he is laughing so hard.

"Why in the world did you bring a baby bonnet all the way to Weihsien?" Tilly asks her.

"It's a very special bonnet. My mother sewed it for me before I was even born. I've always kept it close, and I brought it to Weihsien because I wanted something to remind me of when I was little," Jeanette answers. "Doesn't it look sweet on Albertine?"

Tilly sighs. "Albertine? What kind of name is that for a piglet? Besides, how do you even know it's a girl?"

Miss E. leans over to inspect the piglet's underside. "It is a girl," she says. "But maybe we should vote on her name."

Lu grabs the bucket with the rats inside.

"Do you think he's going to make rat fricassee?" Tilly asks.

"I hope he removes the whiskers. And the eyeballs," Cathy says.

Lu seems to know that the two girls are talking about him. He's been looking out the window. That's when I realize that Lu is as afraid of the Japanese soldiers as we are. He raises his finger to his lips. He's telling us to quiet down. A Japanese soldier is passing outside the hut.

What will happen to Lu if the soldier finds him here?

What will happen to Albertine?

Lu moves away from the window, pressing his back against the wall as if that will help make him disappear if the soldier decides to come inside.

Thank goodness the soldier doesn't stop to check on us. Albertine—the name seems to be sticking—squeals with excitement. Maybe she likes children.

Tilly shakes her head. "She might be cute, but isn't it too risky to have such a noisy creature for a pet?"

Jeanette bites her lip. "Please, Miss E., can't we keep her? Having a pet would be good for our morale."

Miss E.'s eyes soften when Albertine sucks on her finger. "I have a plan," Miss E. says.

FOURTEEN

Albertine is asleep in a box under our pallet, her bonnet slightly rumpled. Miss E.'s plan worked. Besides the eggplant peels Albertine eats for dinner, Miss E. stirs a quarter of a crushed aspirin tablet into the piglet's bowl. We thought Albertine might not like the bitter taste, but she wolfed down her dinner—can you say a piglet *wolfs* down food?—and fell right to sleep. She snores but very quietly.

Tilly, Jeanette and I are gathered around Albertine, admiring her.

"We've only had her four days, and see how she's grown," Jeanette says.

"If she grows too big, we won't be able to keep her inside the hut," Tilly warns.

It isn't easy to leave Albertine. She's such a sweet thing.

But we can't stay with her in the hut all day. We have roll call, work detail and visits to the mess hall. I wonder if it was hard for our parents to leave us at Chefoo. Maybe they also felt they had to—because they were doing the Good Lord's work. Sometimes I feel angry with the Good Lord himself. Why doesn't He put an end to this war and return us to our families?

Lu has been bringing eggplant peels for Albertine. He leaves the scraps in the sandy clearing behind our hut.

"Bye-bye, Albertine." Her snout twitches when I plant a kiss on her hairy, pale-pink belly.

We walk two by two to the mess hall. "It's SOS for lunch," I tell Jeanette, who's next to me.

"SOS? Doesn't that stand for Save Our Souls? What kind of lunch is SOS?" Jeanette sounds excited.

"Same Old Stew!" I tell her.

Dot and Cathy, who are behind us, laugh at my joke, but Jeanette groans. "I was hoping it stood for something delicious. But, of course, you're right, Same Old Stew."

We all line up with our plates or frying pans. Another prisoner, a woman wearing a faded dress, ladles out the stew. It's a pale broth with two tiny eggplant chunks floating in it. When I get out of Weihsien, I know one thing for sure: I will never eat eggplant again. If I even see one at the market, I'll look away.

A Japanese soldier supervises from the corner of the mess hall. I bristle when I realize it's the soldier whose dog I helped. I never told the others about what happened.

Miss E. comes over to the long table where we are sitting on two long, rickety benches. "Doesn't lunch smell divine?" she says.

"Gwendolyn calls it SOS. For Same Old Stew," Dot explains.

Miss E. chuckles. "SOS," she says. "How clever. And funny. It might be the Same Old Stew, but we're glad to have it, aren't we, Girl Guides?"

"Of course we are," several of us say at once.

"A real stew with meat and potatoes would make me gladder," Tilly mutters.

We bow our heads to say grace with Miss E.

There's so little stew that our plates are empty in about a minute. Tilly drags her spoon along the bottom of her frying pan, even though there's nothing left.

"The human brain needs some time to register when we've had a meal, Matilda," Miss E. tells her.

Tilly makes a noise that is somewhere between laughing and crying. She turns to look Miss E. in the eye. "Meal?" she says. "Don't tell me you really think that disgusting SOS counts as a meal. It's water with some rotten eggplant in it."

Now I wonder if the eggplant really was rotten. It did taste worse than usual. My stomach suddenly feels queasy. I didn't know a stomach could feel empty and queasy at the same time.

Miss E. pats Tilly's hand. "Girl Guides smile and sing even in the face of difficulty," she says. "Especially in the face of difficulty." She looks at the rest of us around the table. "Why don't you join me in a song? There's nothing like a little singing to improve one's mood," she says.

"Can we do the chorus of 'Chattanooga Choo Choo'?" Jeanette asks. "It's my favorite part of the song."

Miss E. claps her hands. "That's an excellent suggestion. But we mustn't sing too loudly," she says, glancing at the Japanese soldier.

So we whisper-sing the chorus. Miss E. is right. Even Tilly looks less grumpy, and my stomach feels better.

"*So Chattanooga choo choo, won't you choo-choo me home? Chattanooga choo choo, won't you choo-choo me home?*"

Our singing is interrupted by an angry voice shouting, "*Yameru!*" which is Japanese for "stop."

It's the soldier. At first I think he's heard us singing and wants us to stop. But now I see that his bayonet is raised and he is yelling at one of the coolies.

Miss E.'s face has frozen.

The coolie is our friend Lu.

What has Lu done to upset the guard?

"Look," Dot whispers. "Lu's got a small bucket. I bet you anything he's been collecting scraps for Albertine."

Lu drops the bucket, and a few meager scraps fall on the floor. He bows low to the guard, apologizing in what sounds like a mix of Chinese and Japanese.

But the guard isn't interested in Lu's apology.

When he lifts his bayonet, Miss E. jumps to her feet.

"Don't!" Tilly hisses, pulling Miss E. back to her spot by the bench.

I suck in my breath. Jeanette covers her mouth. Other girls gasp. We're half expecting the soldier to kill Lu on the spot.

But the soldier doesn't use his bayonet to spear Lu to death. Instead he smashes it hard across Lu's face. Lu falls to the floor. There's a river of blood gushing from his nose.

The soldier isn't finished. Before he turns away he kicks Lu in the belly. Not once, not twice, but over and over again.

FIFTEEN

Miss E. always tells us to look on the bright side. Things could have been a lot worse. The guard could have murdered Lu on the spot. "The Good Lord protected him," she tells us afterward, crossing her hands over her heart.

Tilly is not convinced. "If the Good Lord had protected Lu, He wouldn't have let the guard beat him in the first place."

Miss E. gives Tilly a sweet smile. "Well, thank goodness for the black salve I brought from Chefoo," Miss E. says. "It's made from an Asian relative of the bloodroot plant. My uncle Edward believed in the healing powers of bloodroot. It reduces swelling and draws out infection."

Even worse than seeing the guard beat Lu was having to leave Lu lying on the floor of the mess hall as we filed out after lunch. If any of us had tried to help him, we would have been beaten too. But as soon as the coast was clear, Miss E. rushed back to help him. She brought him some of her black salve and applied it to his face. "I'm afraid he'll have a scar along one cheek, but you know, it might actually suit him—it will make him look a little roguish. Besides the scar, I'm sure Lu will make a full recovery. Though he may not be strong enough to bring scraps for Albertine for a few days."

"The Japanese are monsters," Tilly says when Miss E. tells us all this.

"We've talked about this before, Matilda. One shouldn't generalize. It isn't right to say all Japanese are monsters," Miss E. says quietly. "Though I will admit that particular soldier behaved in a monstrous way." It's the first time I've ever heard Miss E. say something bad about another person.

Tilly says she once saw the same soldier kick his own dog.

Miss E. shakes her head in disbelief. "Who would do something like that?" I hear her whisper to herself. Then she waves one hand in the air in front of her as if she doesn't want to think about it. "Let's choose a happier subject," she says. "Which do you like better, Girl Guides—cats or dogs? I don't know why I never thought of asking you this question before."

"Dogs," Jeanette says, "especially puppies with floppy ears."

"But not the dogs here in Weihsien. I'm deathly afraid of them," Dot adds.

Miss E. wags her finger in the air. "Remember the rule. Happy subjects only," she reminds Dot.

"I like cats better," I say. "They're independent. A dog comes if you call him, but a cat, well, a cat does exactly what she wants to."

Later, when Tilly and I are back on cleaning duty in the mess hall, we have to mop up Lu's blood from the floor. I swallow hard when the water in the washing pail turns brownish red.

Poor Lu!

This isn't turning out to be a very good day.

Tilly and I usually have lots to talk about after work, but today we walk back to the hut in silence. I think she is also remembering what happened to Lu—and feeling guilty that he got into trouble for stealing scraps to feed *our* piglet.

When we hear a raspy voice call out "*Ohayo gozaimasu,*" we are so startled we stop in our tracks. Tilly's eyes are as big as saucers, and I can feel my legs turn to jelly. It's another Japanese soldier. This one is taller and older-looking than the others, but he has the same fierce look in his eyes as all the rest. And the bushiest eyebrows I have ever seen.

Did we do something wrong? I can't stop staring at the shiny bayonet hanging at his side. What if he uses it to beat us the way the other soldier beat Lu?

"*Ohayo gozaimasu,*" we answer, bowing from the waist. Does the soldier notice that my legs are shaking?

He gestures for us to follow him. Tilly and I look at each other. I can see in her eyes that she's as nervous as I am. But we know we can't argue with a Japanese soldier. So we follow him down a gravel path through a barren field, which has been picked clean of eggplants. I'm so scared I can feel my heart beating in my throat.

He is leading us to the watchtower at the eastern edge of the camp. What does he want from us?

At first I think he is taking us to the watchtower, but then the soldier makes a sharp turn, and we're in a sandy clearing. Tilly and I stand so close to each other I can hear her breathing. The soldier looks at both of us, then crouches down and opens his arms. He cups his fingers, gesturing for me to come closer.

I suck in my breath.

"Oh, no," I hear Tilly whisper. Her face is gray, and I worry she is going to faint. *Don't faint*, I tell her in my head, hoping she will get the message. *Don't leave me alone with this monster.*

Because I know I don't have a choice, I walk toward the soldier. I take tiny steps, and though he is only a few feet away, it feels as if I am covering a huge distance.

I feel his thick arms wrap around my bony back. I am close enough now to smell his salty skin. So close that if I dared to I could touch his bayonet. I have never felt so afraid. Not even when the Imperial Japanese Army took over our school in Chefoo. Not even when we first arrived at Weihsien. Not even when I thought the German shepherd might maul me.

I close my eyes. In my head I hear Miss E. say, *Try as I might, I may not be able to protect my children.*

Miss E. was right. She can't protect me now.

The soldier lifts me up in the air. What in the world is he doing?

We are close to the electrified gray stone wall, and now I wonder if that's his plan—to throw me high up against the wall so I will end up sizzled and lifeless like Daniel.

I squeeze my eyes tight. I try to think about the Lord—but I can't. Instead I think about Matthew and how it would be a shame to die without ever having experienced true love. It isn't fair. Nothing about life at Weihsien is fair. I clench my fists, because I'm not just scared. I'm also angry.

I half expect to feel a terrible jolt of electricity, but I don't.

Instead I can feel that I am being lifted higher, higher and higher still into the air. I open one eye—just a sliver. My fists unclench. From my one partially opened eye I can see beyond the gates of Weihsien. Now I open both eyes wide.

It has been almost two and a half years since I saw anything except the miserable grounds of this prison.

I see farmers' fields and clumps of small shacks. In the middle is a winding gravel road that leads out toward the horizon. I see a grove of acacia trees. The most amazing thing about my view is that there are no walls anywhere. I forgot what a world without walls looks like. It's as if I can see out to forever.

I laugh so hard my body shakes. I'm laughing because I have not been electrocuted to death, and because for a few minutes I remember what it feels like to be free.

The Japanese soldier laughs with me.

Then Tilly rushes toward us and grabs hold of the soldier's knee. "My turn!" she calls out. "It's my turn now!"

Though I don't think the soldier speaks English, he understands what Tilly is trying to say. Gently he brings me back down to the ground. I land flat and steady on my feet. But in my head I'm still high, high up in the air, enjoying the taste of freedom.

SIXTEEN

"How absolutely wonderful!" Miss E. says when Tilly and I tell her how the Japanese soldier lifted us up so we could see over the stone wall. She closes her eyes as if she is imagining being lifted up by the soldier too. "You must remember that feeling always. And what a kind person to do such a thing." Miss E. turns to look at Tilly. "It goes to show you, Matilda, that not *all* the Japanese are monsters."

As usual, Tilly wants to get in the last word. "If not *all*, then *most*," she says, crossing her arms over her chest.

The other girls want us to tell them more about what we saw. I describe the farmers' fields—the long rows of crops, mostly eggplant and the acacia trees. Tilly describes the run-down shacks. "They're not very fancy, that's for sure," she says

"I wouldn't want to live in one of those shacks," Cathy says.

Dot has been listening, wide eyed. "At least they have their freedom," she says.

"You know what made the biggest impression on me?" I ask the other girls. "That there weren't any walls blocking the view. That the horizon seemed to go on forever. I forgot what a world without walls looks like."

I wish I could make a drawing of what I saw this afternoon. Then I really could remember it always.

Every inch of the sketchpad I brought from Chefoo is full. I keep the sketchpad tucked behind our sleeping pallet, and now, when I take it out, I feel sad as I flip through the pages. I wish I was a better artist. The pad falls open to a sketch of my parents. It was one of my very first drawings. Mother was much prettier in real life, and I had made her lips too thin, and Father...well, there is something wooden about the way I drew him. I did not capture how his eyes lit up, especially when he was preaching. In my head, I suddenly picture Mother and Father when I last saw them. They were delivering me to the boarding school. Mother kissed my forehead. Father shook my hand.

Why is it always so hard to transfer the pictures in my head onto paper?

I think about how Miss E. made us erase our class notes. What if I erased this not-very-good sketch of my parents? I could borrow Miss E.'s eraser, but something stops me. I have never been superstitious. But I have the weird feeling that if I erase this sketch, I'll feel even farther away from my parents than I do already.

I flip through my other sketches. The front entrance of our school in Chefoo with its red double doors. A steaming bowl of dumplings floating in broth (I can't look at that sketch for too long because it makes me so hungry). Miss E. reading from a textbook. In my sketch her cheeks are round and full, and I realize I've forgotten how Miss E. *used* to look when she had enough to eat. I pat my own cheeks and feel the bony parts. Are my cheeks as hollow as Miss E.'s?

I think of how Miss E. would not take any of the crushed-eggshell paste because she said her bones had stopped growing. Or of all the times Miss E. has given one of us a little of her broomcorn or her SOS, saying she's full. Does Miss E. sacrifice some of her food for us?

I think of how hungry I feel at this very second, how I have grown used to the feeling of *always* being hungry, the constant pit in my stomach, the awful dry taste in my mouth. If Miss E. is giving us some of her food, she has to feel even hungrier than we do.

I close my sketchpad, but instead of putting it back behind the pallet, I take it with me outside and sit on the hut's crumbling stone stoop. Usually I like having the other girls to talk to, but right now I want to be alone with my thoughts. Besides, the others are so busy admiring Albertine they won't even notice I've left.

I wish I had a brand-new sketchpad. I pick up a small twig from the ground and spin it between two of my fingers. Maybe it's because the twig is the size of a pencil that I get the idea of using it for drawing. Since I have no sketch paper, I lean forward and use the twig to draw on the gritty earth. I start with a row of small run-down shacks, and then I add some eggplant fields, a cluster of acacia trees and, finally, the long horizon. Drawing the horizon gives me the same feeling of freedom I had when the soldier lifted me up so I could see over the electrified wall.

My drawing will disappear as soon as someone walks over it, or with the next rain. But then I remember something else Miss E. said to me—I will always remember it in my heart. No footsteps or rain can take it away.

Miss E. and Mr. Liddell are walking toward the hut. From where I am sitting I catch bits of their conversation.

"I just don't think it's a wise idea," I hear Mr. Liddell say. What isn't a wise idea?

"It's good for the girls to take care of another living soul," Miss E. tells Mr. Liddell.

Because Miss E. has used the word *soul*, I decide they must be talking about religion.

But then I hear Mr. Liddell say, "When you told me the girls had put a bonnet on that creature, well, that's when I got concerned."

It's Albertine they're talking about—not religion.

Mr. Liddell takes hold of Miss E.'s forearm. "Look how thin your wrists are," he tells her.

Miss E. shakes her arm loose, but she doesn't back away from Mr. Liddell. "I've always had thin wrists," she says.

"That pig—" Mr. Liddell starts to say.

Miss E. interrupts him. "Her name is Albertine."

"That pig—Albertine—is not a doll for you and the girls to play with. That isn't why the coolie gave the creature to you in the first place. That pig is meant for eating. I'm sorry to be so blunt, my dear, but that pig, slaughtered and roasted, might just help keep you and the children alive."

SEVENTEEN

The other girls aren't the only ones who want me to describe the view over the electrified wall. Two days later, after twenty minutes of running on the spot with Mr. Liddell ("It's every bit as good as running on a track," he assures us. "Lift those knees, ladies and gents!"), Matthew says he wants to speak to me.

I wipe the sweat from my forehead. Mr. Liddell is right that running on the spot is good exercise. There are giant wet rings under Matthew's armpits, and his forehead is sweaty too, but he doesn't bother wiping it.

"Is it about books?" I ask Matthew. "Or rats?"

"Neither," he says. "Why don't we go for a little walk? So we can have some privacy."

I blush when Matthew says that. Wait till I tell Tilly and Jeanette. They probably won't even believe that a boy like Matthew has invited *me* to go for a walk with him. I'm just a regular girl. Nowhere near as beautiful as Jeanette or with as much personality as Tilly. Why would Matthew want to talk to a girl like me?

What will I do if he tries to hold my hand? Shake his hand loose the way I saw Miss E. do with Mr. Liddell? Or let Matthew hold my hand—and maybe even squeeze his back?

I am disappointed when Matthew does *not* try to hold my hand. We walk down the gravel path that leads away from the girls' and boys' huts. I am also disappointed that we don't run into Tilly or Jeanette—or any of the girls, who would definitely tell Tilly and Jeanette if they saw me with Matthew.

"I heard that you and Tilly made friends with a soldier, and that he lifted you up so you could see over the stone wall," Matthew says.

"Who told you that?"

"Word spreads quickly at Weihsien" is all Matthew will say. "It's important for us to pay attention to things."

"Us?" I ask Matthew. "Who's *us*?"

For a moment Matthew looks like he's been trapped. But then he shrugs and says, "You know, everyone in the camp."

"I drew a picture afterward," I tell Matthew. "There wasn't room left in my sketchpad. So I drew it on the ground." I don't know why I want him to know all this.

I can tell from the way Matthew is watching my face that he is interested in what I am saying. It makes me want to tell him more. "The rain washed my drawing away."

"I would have liked to see it," Matthew says.

"Really?" I run my fingers over my *Artist* badge. Should I show it to him? Or would he think I was showing off? But then I decide I want him to know about the badge and about this part of me. "This is my newest badge," I tell him.

"Artist," he says. "Congratulations. I've heard Miss E. doesn't part easily with her badges."

I don't tell Matthew that I wish I was a better artist. "You're right," I say. "Miss E. doesn't part easily with her badges. But she said the drawing I made of our school in Chefoo gave her shivers."

"Shivers," Matthew says. "That's saying something." His arm brushes against mine, and I nearly tell him that I am having shivers. Does he have them too?

"Gwen, could you tell me about what you saw over the wall?" Matthew asks.

I tell him what I told the others—about the run-down shacks, the eggplant fields, the grove of acacia trees, and how good it felt to see a world without walls.

Matthew stops walking and turns to face me. "What about a road?" he asks. "Did you see a road?"

"Um, I'm not sure."

"Close your eyes and try to remember," Matthew tells me.

I do what Matthew says. Even with my eyes closed I can feel Matthew standing across from me.

"A road," he says again. "Was there a road?"

That's when something else comes back to me. "There was a road," I tell him, opening my eyes. "A narrow gravel road. Behind the rows of eggplant."

"Which way did it go?"

"Why do you care so much about a road?"

"It's better not to ask too many questions, Gwen."

"You ask a lot of questions!"

That makes Matthew laugh. "I guess that's true. Now which way did the road go? Away from the sea or alongside it? Does it run north-south or east-west?"

Something about the way Matthew asks these questions makes me nervous. As if it's a test I didn't study for. "I'm not sure. It was hard to tell north from south or east from west. But like I said, the road was behind the fields. Definitely."

Matthew squats down on the ground and gestures for me to squat next to him. "Can you draw it for me?"

I'm a little disappointed that Matthew does not compliment the way I draw the shacks and the eggplant fields. He's only interested in the road. He runs his finger over the lines I've made on the ground. "So the road runs north-south. Hmm. That's good to know. Thank you, Gwen."

Now something else comes back to me. It's strange that I'm only remembering it now. There was a cemetery near the road. I know because I saw the headstones. I tell Matthew about the cemetery. He wants to know how close it was to the road.

I point to a spot on the drawing I made on the ground.

"Hmm," he says again. "Interesting. That could be useful."

"Useful for what?" I ask.

"I told you it was better not to ask too many questions."

"I can't help it. It's how my mind works."

That makes Matthew laugh, which makes me laugh. "I like how your mind works, Gwen," he says. And even if he did not compliment my drawing, I'm glad he likes how my mind works and also that he thinks I'm funny. Matthew uses the heel of his boot to erase my drawing. "We wouldn't want anyone else to see it," he says.

I decide not to ask him why. I come up with another question instead—one I know he won't mind answering. "How's the book?"

"What book?"

"*Around the World in Eighty Days*. The one you borrowed from the lending library. You said you couldn't wait to read it."

"It's excellent—so far. I haven't had much time to read."

"Miss E. says it's important to make time for reading. Even if we only read for a few minutes a day."

"Miss E. says a lot of things."

Something about the way Matthew says that bothers me. "I adore Miss E.," I tell him. "When I grow up I want to be just like her."

"Is it true you've got a piglet in your hut?" Matthew asks.

My mind flashes on the picture of Matthew with the dead rat in his arms. "You really do ask a lot of questions," I tell him.

"That means you *are* keeping a piglet in your hut."

"I never said that."

"That's true. You didn't say it. You're not a very good liar, are you, Gwen?"

"You're right. I'm not. But it doesn't matter because I'm against lying. Miss E. is against it too. Girl Guides always tell the truth."

"Are you also against eating that piglet once it's fattened up and full grown?"

"Of course I am."

Matthew claps his hands. There's laughter in his eyes. "So you've admitted it. You do have a piglet in your hut."

I decide it's better not to say anything. For a moment Matthew and I just look at each other. He's the one who breaks the silence. "Aren't you starving like the rest of us?" he asks. "And don't you dream of getting out of here?" This time, there's no laughter in Matthew's eyes.

EIGHTEEN

Mr. Liddell rubs his hands together as if he is going to share some great news. "The beauty of the exercise I'm about to teach you," he says, "is that no one will even know you're doing it." Maybe it's the way the sun is landing on Mr. Liddell, but his face looks thinner and more lined than ever.

Tilly doesn't raise her hand before she asks a question. "Does that mean we can do it at roll call?"

Mr. Liddell pauses before he answers. "As a matter of fact, it does."

"Well, show it to us then!" Amos calls out.

"Manners!" Miss E. tells Amos, wagging her finger in the air. "How lucky are we all to know an Olympic champion?"

"Mr. Liddell, would you show us the exercise, *please*?" Amos says, correcting himself.

Miss E. nods approvingly.

"What you have to do is clench your buttocks," Mr. Liddell explains. He turns around to demonstrate.

"Buttocks!" several voices call out. And we all start to laugh. Who knew there was an exercise for the buttocks?

Mr. Liddell and Miss E. exchange a look. I think they are deciding whether to reprimand us for laughing. In the end they must decide against it. I have a feeling Miss E. thinks laughter is as important as good manners and being cheerful.

Mr. Liddell waits for us to settle down. "Now let's clench our buttocks. There's nothing to be embarrassed about, ladies and gents. This is an excellent exercise for strengthening the gluteus maximus muscle. All together now! We clench for ten seconds. We'll do three sets of eight."

Miss E. raises one finger in the air. "What do we get when we multiply three times eight?" Leave it to Miss E. to teach us arithmetic during gym class.

Matthew raises his hand. He waits for Miss E. to nod before he answers her question. I like that Matthew has good manners. "Twenty-four!" he says.

"Very good. And what about four times eight?" Miss E. asks.

Mr. Liddell turns to look directly at Miss E. "Four times eight makes thirty-two," he tells her. "Now if you don't mind, I'd like these youngsters to concentrate on muscle training. I don't ask them to clench their buttocks when you are teaching them geography or how to write haiku!"

Their argument makes us laugh some more. Of course we all know that Mr. Liddell and Miss E. aren't really arguing. Only teasing each other the way friends do.

"We'll do some calf raises next," Mr. Liddell says. "I want you all to squat down for this exercise. Be careful not to bump into each other. We're in rather close quarters. I'll demonstrate from the bench."

Mr. Liddell sighs when he sits down on the small wooden bench. For an Olympic athlete, he seems unusually tired. Then again, like all of us, he's getting very little to eat. And because he's so tall, he must need even more food than we do. "I want you to put all your weight on the tips of your toes. Like this. We'll hold for ten seconds. Eight repetitions. And yes, Miss E., I think we all know that ten times eight is eighty."

By the third repetition I can feel my calf muscles burning.

"Eight, nine, nine and a half, nine and three quarters..." Mr. Liddell calls out. Next to me, Jeanette is wincing. Cathy, who is next to Jeanette, isn't having any trouble doing the exercise. I know because she waves when she sees me looking at her.

Mr. Liddell gets up from the bench. Because we are packed in so tightly, there isn't much room for him when he comes to check on us. "Tip those toes a little more forward!" he tells Benton.

"Excellent work," he says to Cathy. "Your calves will be sore tomorrow—but it's the best kind of sore."

I tip so far forward I'm afraid I'll crash into Eunice, who is in front of me. My calf muscles are shaking.

I hope Mr. Liddell will compliment me too.

But when I peek at Mr. Liddell I notice that his eyes have a glassy look and his forehead is all sweaty. "Mr. Liddell, are you all r—" I start to ask.

Mr. Liddell looks surprised that someone has spoken to him. When he suddenly collapses, my first thought is that it's my fault, that I've startled him.

Miss E. rushes over. Mr. Liddell is lying on the ground, his eyes closed. I know he isn't dead because I can see his chest moving lightly up and down as he breathes. He is so thin that his ribs jut out from underneath his white shirt.

"Someone run to the infirmary for some water!" Miss E. calls out. She slides one arm under Mr. Liddell's neck. "Eric," she says in a louder than usual voice, "you've overexerted yourself with today's gym class. But everything is going to be fine."

A few minutes later Matthew comes back with some water from the infirmary. There's usually a little fresh water there in case of emergency. "Small sips only," Miss E. tells Mr. Liddell.

Miss E. makes an announcement from her spot on the floor. "Girls and boys," she says, "gym class is ending earlier than expected. May I suggest you use this time to review your geography notes or work on your haikus? And perhaps a couple of you could help me get

Mr. Liddell to the infirmary. Not that there's anything wrong with him, of course. We just want him seen to."

Tilly tugs on my tunic. "There is definitely something wrong with Mr. Liddell," she whispers.

"Miss E. says he overexerted himself."

Tilly shakes her head and looks at me as if I'm an idiot. "I don't understand why you keep believing every word Miss E. says. An Olympic athlete—even one who isn't getting enough to eat—does not overexert himself by standing on his tippy-toes. Or sitting on a bench."

I hate to admit it, but in my heart I know Tilly is right.

NINETEEN

We call it the infirmary, but in the same way the lending library isn't much of a library, the infirmary at Weihsien isn't much of an infirmary.

It's a crumbling old building with broken windows, and rows of narrow iron cots inside. Some of the cots are separated by gray curtains that were probably once white. Most of the curtains are missing, though, taken down and used for clothing. Sometimes I notice women in boxy-looking gray dresses made from infirmary curtains.

But as Miss E. is always reminding us, it helps to look on the bright side. The bright side is that the infirmary has a doctor. A real doctor. Dr. McGregor was working in a clinic outside Chefoo when the Japanese invaded China. Because the Japanese sent all foreign nationals from around Chefoo to internment camps, and Dr. McGregor is Scottish, he ended up in Weihsien too. He is a small man with a beaky nose. He wears thick eyeglasses held together in the middle by a piece of frayed wire. Every time I see those glasses, I find myself hoping that Dr. McGregor does neater work when he stitches up a wound.

We follow Miss E. and Mr. Liddell to the infirmary, but Miss E. shoos us away when we get there. So we wait outside for news. I've never been good at waiting, but I'm getting better. I get a lot of practice at Weihsien. We wait for our broomcorn and SOS, we wait for roll call to be over, we wait to use the latrine. And, of course, we wait for this war to end.

"I hope they'll find something for Mr. Liddell to eat," I say to the others. "He's even skinnier than we are."

Jeanette nods. "Mr. Liddell overexerted himself. That's what Miss E. said."

Matthew and Benton are also waiting for news. I can't help flinching when a Japanese soldier walks by. His eyes scan over us, and I think we are all a little bit surprised— and a lot relieved—when he does not order us to go back to our huts. Maybe he knows Mr. Liddell collapsed, and he understands that we're worried about our friend.

I'm disappointed that Matthew doesn't come to sit near me. I thought we were friends. When I give him the smallest smile, he doesn't smile back. Something pinches in my chest near where my heart is. He's acting like he doesn't even know me. I'm glad I never told Jeanette and Tilly that he asked me to go for a walk with him.

I make a point of *not* looking at Matthew. Only that's harder than it sounds. Not only because I think I like him, but also because when you try *not* to look at someone it only makes you want to look at them more.

"I see Miss E.," Cathy says, pointing to a small, cracked window near the front of the infirmary. Through the window we make out Miss E. talking with Dr. McGregor, their heads bowed. Miss E. is chewing on her finger.

"Maybe Mr. Liddell is dying," Tilly blurts out.

I could smack her for saying that. "Of course he isn't dying," I tell her.

"Dr. McGregor is very good. He'll fix whatever is wrong with Mr. Liddell," Jeanette adds.

"What Mr. Liddell needs is food and water," Matthew says, joining in the conversation. I forget my plan not to look at him, but when I do I get the strangest feeling that he is making a point of not looking at *me*. Did I do something to upset him? Maybe he thinks I talk too much. "We all need food and water," Matthew adds, "or we'll end up collapsing too."

The door to the infirmary opens, and Miss E. comes out. She seems surprised to find us there. Her lips are pursed, but when she sees us, her face relaxes.

"Is he going to die?" Tilly asks.

When Tilly's question makes Miss E. laugh, I know for sure everything is going to be fine. "Mr. Liddell isn't going to die. Not for a very long time anyway." Miss E. ruffles Tilly's hair. "You can stop worrying, Matilda. Dr. McGregor says Mr. Liddell has a touch of influenza. All Mr. Liddell needs is some rest—and something to eat."

Benton puts his hands on his hips. "Where exactly does the doctor plan to find something for Mr. Liddell to eat?" he asks.

Miss E. doesn't answer Benton's question. She just moves so quickly to a new topic it's hard to remember the old one. She does that a lot.

"I think you'll like my latest idea. Have you ever noticed that good ideas come at the oddest times? I got this particular idea while Dr. McGregor was rattling on about his childhood in Scotland while he was examining Mr. Liddell."

"What was your idea?" Tilly asks.

Miss E.'s eyes are dancing in a way that makes me think she is playing with us. She claps her hands together. "Cards," she says. "Get-well cards. Imagine how much Mr. Liddell would enjoy getting a card from each of you."

"But there's no paper left," Tilly says. "We've already erased our notebooks."

"I wasn't thinking of paper cards," Miss E. says. "I was thinking of musical ones. What if each of you prepared a small get-well song for Mr. Liddell? Then in a few days, once he's feeling stronger, we could have a musical performance in his honor."

"I'll play the flute," Jeanette says.

"I was going to suggest that myself," Miss E. says.

"Can we bring Albertine?" Jeanette wants to know. "She could wear her bonnet."

Miss E. continues speaking as if she hasn't heard Jeanette. "Rather than inventing new songs, you could take ones you already know and change the words. For instance, *He was a famous trumpet man from out Chicago way* could be *He was a Scottish doctor from Ed-in-burgh…*"

On our way back to the huts we have lots to talk about. Between us, we must know fifty different songs. "What about 'Take My Hand, Precious Lord'?" Matthew suggests. "We could change it to 'Run This Race, Olympic Champ.'"

Jeanette puts one hand over her heart. "I don't think Mr. Liddell would like us mocking a religious song. It could slow down his recovery. Why don't you think of something else?"

Though I swear I didn't plan it, Matthew and I end up walking side by side.

When he doesn't say a word to me, I feel that pinch in my chest again. I will not be the one to start a conversation. If Matthew is ignoring me, I'll ignore him.

That plan works as well as my plan not to look at him.

"I don't know why you're ignoring me," I blurt out. As soon as the words have left my mouth, I wish I could take them back.

Matthew glances to the left and to the right, then in front and behind. When he speaks, his voice is so low I have to lean in to hear him. "I'm sorry, Gwen. Trust me—it's for the best."

For the best? What are you talking about? You can't just go and ignore a girl you invited for a walk.

But I don't say that out loud. I just think it. Because although I have no idea what Matthew means, something tells me this isn't a good time to argue about it.

TWENTY

Jeanette is singing us a song that was one of her mother's favorites. "It's called 'On the Sunny Side of the Street.'" She swivels her shoulders as she sings a verse. *"Grab your coat and get your hat. Leave your worries on the doorstep."*

We are so busy learning the song and planning how to change it for Mr. Liddell's musical card (*"Grab your mosquito net. Don't forget your plate. Leave your worries at Weihsien"*) that we don't even notice Miss E. has come into our hut. She doesn't clap to get our attention the way she usually does. She just waits for us to notice that she's standing by the door.

"We have to discuss something serious." That's when I realize that in all the time Miss E. has been looking after us, she has never talked to us about something serious. Even when she teaches us geography or literature, she finds a way to turn it into a game.

"Is it about Mr. Liddell?" Tilly asks.

"It is about him. In a way," Miss E. says. I'm so used to seeing Miss E. smile that seeing her now, without any smile at all, feels all wrong. Like I am traveling to a place I've never been—like when we boarded the steamer and then the train that brought us here to Weihsien.

"Is he dead?" Tilly asks.

"Mr. Liddell isn't dead," Miss E. assures us. "People don't die from influenza."

"They do too. My grandmother died of it," Tilly insists.

"Well, they don't *usually*," Miss E. says. "But the thing is, as you know"—when Miss E. pauses, something tells me she needs courage to continue—"Mr. Liddell is very, very weak. He needs more food. I hoped it would never come to this, girls, but I'm going to have to… to… " Miss E. lets her voice trail off.

"Kill Alb—" Tilly starts to say.

Miss E. stretches out her arm and raises her palm in the air. I think she doesn't want Tilly to have to say it. "I'm going to have to slaughter Albertine." Miss E.'s eyes are shiny, but she isn't crying. "I hoped it wouldn't come to this, Girl Guides, I really did. And I think it's been good for you to look after another…creature. I know, of course, that you'll want to say your goodbyes."

I put my hand over my mouth.

Jeanette lets out a loud sob.

When I put my arm around Jeanette's shoulders I feel how bony she has become. She feels more like a bird than a girl. And though I'm also sorry about the news, I can't help wondering, Will we get something extra to eat too, after Albertine is killed?

Tilly makes a harrumphing sound. "Albertine isn't a human baby," she says. "Even if she wears a bonnet. She's a pig, and pigs are made for eating. It's only too bad that she isn't fully grown. We'd get more meat if we could let her live longer."

Miss E. swallows before she speaks. "Dr. McGregor doesn't think we can wait much longer. Mr. Liddell needs to eat something more substantial than broomcorn and eggplant."

"Who's going to kill her?" I ask.

Miss E. looks me in the eye without blinking. "Me."

Tilly and Jeanette get into an argument about whether we should remove Albertine's bonnet before we say our goodbyes. "I want to remember her with her bonnet on," Jeanette insists.

"You can remember her any way you want," Tilly says in an irritated voice. "But the sooner we stop thinking about Albertine as a pet, the easier it will be to let her go." When Tilly does not use the word *kill* or *slaughter*, I understand that saying goodbye to Albertine will be hard for Tilly too—even if she doesn't want the rest of us to know it.

"When are you going to...to do it?" I ask Miss E.

"As soon as I can get the right"—Miss E. stops to choose her words—"equipment. Hopefully by tonight. It might be easier," she adds, "without the bonnet."

We follow Miss E. to Albertine's enclosed pen behind our hut. Albertine has quadrupled in size in the three weeks we've had her. She's not as big as a German shepherd, more the size of a bulldog. She's sound asleep (thanks to her daily dose of aspirin), but now she opens one yellowish-brown eye. "I'm going to take off her bonnet," Miss E. says to Jeanette. "Maybe you'd like to have one last look at her with her bonnet on."

Jeanette shakes her head.

Miss E. takes a deep breath. "Albertine," she says, "we're grateful to have had your wonderful company. You've brightened all our spirits during a difficult time. Not only have you made us laugh with your antics, but you've taught us about the importance of caring for others. We're especially grateful that you are giving your life to save Mr. Liddell's." Miss E. leans over to kiss Albertine's head. As she does, she begins to recite the Twenty-Third Psalm: *"The Lord is my shepherd, I shall not want…"*

Because it's a psalm we all know, we join in. *"He maketh me to lie down in green pastures…"*

When we finish, Miss E. takes another deep breath. "Who wants to go next?"

Because I want to help Miss E., I say I will. Though I always thought it was Miss E.'s job to look after us, I am starting to realize that sometimes even someone as strong, brave and independent as Miss E. needs to be looked after too. "Goodbye, Albertine," I say. Though it's hard to do, I look her in the eye—the way Miss E. looked at me before.

Albertine returns my gaze in a way that makes me think she understands what's going to happen to her. Then I crouch down and lower my voice so only Albertine can hear. "I'm awfully sorry."

Jeanette takes her turn next. I think we're all expecting a long, tearful speech. But all Jeanette does is scratch behind one of Albertine's ears. When Albertine grunts, Jeanette grunts back. Albertine grunts again, and for a moment I wonder if that grunt could mean *goodbye*.

Tilly waits for all the other girls to say goodbye before she takes her turn. "To be honest," she says, "I don't know why the others are making such a fuss about you." I notice she isn't using Albertine's name. "Pigs are not meant to be pets. They are meant to be slaughtered and eaten."

If, at that very moment, Tilly did not use the back of her hand to wipe her cheek, I might never have guessed that even Tilly—who is the most practical and sensible girl I ever knew—also loved Albertine.

TWENTY-ONE

Some nights the bedbugs won't let me sleep. Mostly, though, it's the hunger and the thirst that keep me up. When your belly is empty and your throat is parched, it's hard to think of anything else besides food and fresh water.

Jeanette says fasting purifies the soul. "Actually, I didn't say it. St. Augustine did. He also said that fasting makes the heart contrite and humble."

Tilly rolls her eyes. "Even St. Augustine might change his mind if he was at Weihsien. He might just abandon his fast for a juicy pork chop."

"Tilly! How can you say that?" Jeanette and I ask at the same time.

Somehow, even with the bedbugs, my empty belly, my parched throat and Tilly's pork chop joke, I can feel myself starting to doze off. My arms and legs get heavy, and I let my head slump a little to one side. Before I came to Weihsien I used to hate falling asleep. When I was small I'd beg my parents to let me stay up even half an hour later so I could draw. But now, on the nights I'm able to doze off, I'm so grateful I could cry. Probably because it means that for at least a few hours I can be somewhere else.

The last thing I see are Albertine's yellowish-brown eyes. I tell myself that Albertine, who has never done a selfish thing or had a selfish thought in all her life (not that I know of anyhow), will go to heaven. I just hope that the Lord will forgive my many selfish thoughts and that I will get there too. If I do, I'll get to play with Albertine again. She is the best pig I ever met.

Maybe tonight I'll dream about a better world. The air there will never be muggy. The sky will always be blue. There will be cupboards full of good things to eat— and books to read and vellum paper to draw on. Best of all, I will get to be with the people I love most—Miss E., my friends from Weihsien and even my mother and father. Though I often feel angry with them for leaving me in Chefoo, I can't seem to stop loving them. Not even when I try. Is that what love is? When you can't stop loving a person even when you want to?

As I begin to fall into a deeper, heavier sleep, I see them—my mother and father. They are sitting at the dining room table, heads bowed, hands pressed together as Father says grace. Mother mouths the words along with him.

There is the white lace tablecloth Mother brought with her from Boston. It was a wedding gift from her parents. "It will be yours one day, Gwen," she used to say when she spread it out on the table.

When the prayer is finished, Mother and Father look up at each other and smile. Then they reach for their chopsticks. They are having dumplings and a plate of baby bok choy and oyster mushrooms for supper. Clouds of steam rise from their blue-and-white porcelain bowls and disappear into the air. Father catches a dumpling between his chopsticks, blowing on it before he takes a bite.

Something makes Mother and Father laugh. Mother's laugh sounds like wind chimes. Father's is a low rumble.

What's so funny?

Now I notice that someone else is sitting with them at the table, her chopsticks lying side by side on my tablecloth.

It's a girl, and she is sitting in the spot where I should be—between my parents. Her hair is silky black and perfectly straight. When she moves it away from her face, I see from the shape of her eyes that she is Chinese.

"Father...Mother," I hear the girl say.

They're not *her* parents. They are *mine*.

I'm sure my parents will explain that she's mistaken. But they don't. "This tablecloth will be yours one day," I hear my mother tell the girl.

"But shouldn't it go to Gwen?" the girl asks.

"Gwen?" My parents exchange a confused look. "Who's Gwen?"

My mother looks up into the air. Where, I wonder, is the red-and-gold silk lantern that hung over the dining room table at our house in Chefoo?

Where are the walls? The ceiling? Why is there a perfectly blue sky inside my parents' dining room?

The sky is bluer than a robin's egg. I don't know where my parents went or the Chinese girl who was sitting in my spot. It doesn't matter. I'll find them later and explain that I'm their daughter Gwen. I'll make the girl understand that the tablecloth belongs to me.

Now I'm suddenly spinning around and around, faster and faster, like a toy top. It feels so good to laugh. I'm not worried that I'll fall because I can feel the Japanese soldier's strong, sturdy arms around me. *Pay attention*, a boy's voice tells me. *Do you see a road? Does it go north-south or east-west? Pay attention, Gwen.*

Why do I hear dogs snarling and barking? Why are voices shouting in Japanese?

If it's the middle of the night, why are there lanterns burning?

What in the world is going on?

This isn't our old house in Chefoo, and this definitely isn't a better world.

Next to me Jeanette groans in her sleep. On my other side Tilly is sitting bolt upright.

"What do you think is going on out there?" I ask her.

"I think there's been an escape," she says.

Cathy and Dot are awake now too. "An escape?" Cathy asks, rubbing the sleep from her eyes.

"That's impossible," I tell Tilly. "Nobody escapes from Weihsien. Not with all the soldiers. And the electrified stone wall."

"Impossible?" Tilly says. "I thought you and your beloved Miss E. didn't believe in that word!"

TWENTY-TWO

We don't sleep after that. Not only because of the barking dogs, the shouting guards and our own excitement, but also because the bells for roll call are sounding.

"It's pitch dark," Jeanette says, rubbing her eyes. "They can't make us line up for roll call now."

"They can make us do anything they want," Tilly tells her.

So even though it's the middle of the night, we put on our Girl Guide uniforms. We don't bother with the pale-blue scarves.

When we head for the area behind the mess hall to report for roll call, none of us says a word. There are Japanese soldiers and snarling dogs everywhere. I think we're all wondering the same thing. How could anyone have escaped from this place?

Two Japanese soldiers jump onto the back of an army truck. One of them smacks the back of the truck with his bayonet, and the truck takes off in the direction of the main gate to the camp. A dog howls from inside the truck.

A second army truck follows. Someone shouts orders in Japanese. Whoever it is sounds angry.

The main gates open and the trucks sputter, then pick up speed as they roll down the road. We all know the soldiers' mission—to return to Weihsien with whoever has managed to escape. I shudder to think about what will happen when they find the person. The last time there was an escape from Weihsien was before our arrival. But we've all heard the story of what happened to the man who escaped. The Japanese found him and brought him back to Weihsien in chains. Then they gathered all the prisoners to watch as they forced the man to dig his own grave, then shot him and threw him into the grave he'd dug. I'm glad I wasn't there to see it.

Whoever escaped must be as weak and hungry as the rest of us. The Japanese soldiers will find him—or her.

"Where's Miss E.?" Eunice asks.

Eunice's question sends a shiver down my spine. Could Miss E. have been the one to escape? I can't believe I even thought that! Miss E. would never abandon us. Ever. Not the way our parents did.

Just as I'm thinking that, Miss E. appears—almost out of nowhere, her eyes glowing like an owl's.

Miss E. does not bother saying hello. But that doesn't matter. What matters is that she is here with us.

Together we line up for roll call. We cannot look around too much because we don't want to make the Japanese guards any angrier than they already are. But we all want to know the same thing. Who was foolish—or brave—enough to attempt an escape from Weihsien?

It was probably one of the older men. Maybe someone who found a way to hide some money and who speaks Chinese. Someone like that could bribe a coolie into helping him. Because if there is one thing I know it's that no one could escape from Weihsien without help.

But the older men and women report to a different spot for roll call. Where we go, it's mostly just the children from Chefoo and our teachers. I see the Japanese soldier with his tally book. Behind me I hear someone yawn, which makes me want to yawn too. But I know I can't. The air feels muggier than ever—as if the tension in the camp is making the atmospheric pressure drop even lower.

In the distance I hear dogs snarling. Have they already caught the escapee? Of course I hope not. What if they make whoever it is dig his own grave and shoot him in front of all of us? I don't think I could bear it. Though I'm mostly glad that someone had the brains and the courage to get out of here, a small part of me resents whoever it is. If it weren't for him—or her—the rest of us would get another hour or two of sleep! Even swatting lice and bedbugs is better than standing here in the pitch dark.

The Japanese soldier who's in charge clicks his boots together, and we start calling out our numbers. More soldiers turn up—with dogs. The dogs' ears are pricked. They know something serious is going on. A few dogs circulate among us, sniffing our ankles as if they are hunting for clues.

Even if I could look behind me, I wouldn't. I never want Matthew to catch me looking at him again. Not after the way he ignored me in front of the others. I'm better off pretending that Matthew doesn't exist, that he never laughed when I called him a rat catcher and that he never asked me to go with him for a walk.

Ichi, ni, san....

Miss E. is staring forward in the strangest way. A muscle in her right cheek twitches.

Tilly nudges me with her elbow. I want to ask her what she's thinking—this is roll call, and the Japanese soldiers are even angrier than usual! We could be severely punished for any kind of misbehavior.

Tilly nudges me again. She wants me to look at her, but I won't. Whatever it is she wants to tell me will have to wait till roll call is over. If it's ever over. I'm so tired it's hard to keep my head from rolling to one side.

Then I hear the tiniest whisper. It sounds more like air than words. "*It's Matthew and Benton.*"

I forget all about the promise I just made to never let Matthew catch me looking at him again. But it doesn't really matter, because when I turn around, Matthew and Benton are not in their usual spots.

I can almost feel the savage kick in the legs that will be coming to me. I bite down on my lip as if I can already feel the pain.

But no one kicks me in the legs. That's because the Japanese soldiers seem to have realized which of the prisoners have escaped. I hear the soldiers whispering.

Miss E. is still staring straight ahead, but at least her cheek has stopped twitching. One Japanese soldier yells out orders, and the soldier with the tally book marches off toward the main gate. Another soldier is already heading for the guardhouse.

Matthew and Benton! How did they manage it?

Please, Lord, keep Matthew safe—and Benton too. Please, Lord, do not let the Japanese soldiers catch the two boys.

At least now we can return to our hut. Even though I know I'll never get another wink of sleep before morning.

But the Japanese soldiers don't let us go back to our sleeping pallets.

Instead they make us do roll call a second time—and when we are finished they make us do it over again. And then again. A dog bares his teeth at Jeanette, but she swallows her scream.

We are being punished for the boys' escape.

I am more tired and hungry than I have ever been. In a strange way it feels like I'm already dead. No, I tell myself, death would feel better than this.

Miss E. taught us that horses can sleep standing up. I didn't know people could do it too. But I can feel my eyes getting heavy—I am starting to doze off. I am jolted suddenly awake when a boy in the row behind me is too tired to call his number and is rewarded with a kick in the shins. When he cries out in pain, the boy earns a second kick. This time he doesn't cry out.

I see the fear in the other girls' eyes. Cathy chews on her fingernail. The others are as afraid as I am that they will fall asleep and be too tired to call out their numbers.

The fear keeps me awake—but only for a while.

I can't keep track of the number of roll calls we have done. Is it six or seven? Or maybe eight? I am so tired I am keeling over.

Far away I hear the sounds of children counting in Japanese. My head slumps to the side.

I have to stay awake, but I can't fight it anymore. My head slumps lower...oh, it feels so good to close my eyes...and then, out of nowhere, something furry nudges my ankle. The feeling startles me, and I am awake. Just in time to call out my number.

I look down. A dog is crouched on the ground by my feet. When our eyes meet, I realize it's the German shepherd whose paw had the piece of glass in it.

When his tail wags, it thumps against my ankle. I think he's glad he found a way to return the good turn I did for him.

TWENTY-THREE

I never dreamed that I would look forward to broomcorn. But when the first pale pink rays of the sun peek up over the horizon and the Japanese soldiers finally stop the endless roll call, all I can think about is broomcorn. We are so exhausted we can barely walk in a straight line.

Jeanette rests her head on my shoulder. I don't have the energy to tell her that her head is too heavy and she needs to move it. "Do you think they'll let us get some sleep before work detail?" she asks.

"Of course they *won't*," Tilly answers for me.

"We'll feel better once we eat our broomcorn," I tell Jeanette. I can almost feel the flavorless mush in my mouth and the way it will make the awful empty pit in my stomach a little less deep.

"What do you want to bet we don't get broomcorn either?" Tilly asks.

When she says it, I suddenly realize she's right. Forcing us to do roll call until dawn could be just the appetizer before the main course. I need to stop thinking about food.

Miss E. has been listening in on our conversation. "Girl Guides," she says in a voice that doesn't sound at all tired, "this is simply one more challenge for us to face with dignity and good cheer. Let's make a game of it!"

Tilly rubs her eyes with the backs of her hands. "How are we supposed to make a game of being tired and hungry?" she asks.

"Let's imagine feeling exactly the opposite. What if we'd just had a wonderful night's sleep and so much to eat that we could hardly walk?" Miss E. asks.

"I can hardly walk because I haven't slept and because I'm so hungry," Jeanette says.

"That isn't the game," I tell Jeanette. "Miss E. wants us to imagine things being completely opposite to what they are. I'll do it."

"Of course you will," Tilly mutters under her breath. "You'd jump off a bridge if Miss E. told you to."

"I wouldn't."

"You would so."

"Girl Guides!" Miss E. says.

It's hard to know whether Miss E. is telling us to stop arguing, or whether she is alerting us to the fact that there are two Japanese soldiers up ahead. Tilly and I let our argument drop. One of the soldiers is speaking loudly into a transmission device. Even though I don't understand Japanese, I can tell from his tone that he is upset. I hope it means Matthew and Benton have not been caught.

I think we're all relieved that the soldiers don't even bother to look at us. Still, we wait until we're well past them before we say another word.

"Did you understand any of what they were saying?" Tilly asks Miss E. It's a good question. Miss E. isn't fluent in Japanese, but she does know quite a few words.

"I think I got the gist of it," Miss E. answers. "They can't figure out how the boys managed to escape." Is it my imagination, or do I see one of Miss E.'s dimples make a brief appearance?

"How do you think they did it?" Jeanette asks Miss E.

"I haven't the faintest idea," Miss E. says, crossing her arms over her chest. "They might have dug a trench. Or... used a ladder. But based on what I managed to pick up from the conversation, the soldiers can't find any evidence. It must not feel very good to be an Imperial soldier with a shiny bayonet and have been outsmarted by two scrawny fifteen-year-olds." There's the dimple again. I'm sure I saw it this time.

"What will they do to the boys if they catch them?" Jeanette asks.

"They won't catch them," Miss E. says.

"They'll kill them. And hang them upside down to dry. Or make them dig their own graves and shoot them. All to teach a lesson to the rest of us," Tilly says.

"Matilda!" Miss E. says sharply—and for a moment I think Miss E. is going to lose her temper. But then she pinches Tilly's ear and says, "Perhaps, Matilda, you could apply that wild imagination of yours to the game I suggested before. Go ahead and tell us where you'd be if you'd had a delicious night's sleep and way too much to eat."

The last thing I expect is that Tilly will play along. But she does. Maybe Tilly is tired of being cranky. "I'd be at Buckingham Palace," she says. "I'd sleep on a solid-gold bed with a feather mattress. And I'd have roast beef and Yorkshire pudding for breakfast, lunch and supper."

Miss E. laughs. "Mmm," she says. "I can practically taste the roast beef and Yorkshire pudding. Dee-licious. What about you, Jeanette and Gwen? If your stomachs could be full to bursting with anything, what would it be?"

"Apple pie with vanilla ice cream." Jeanette has closed her eyes, and her voice sounds dreamy. "For breakfast, lunch and supper."

"You stole that line from me!" Tilly says.

"Well then, take it as a compliment," Miss E. tells Tilly.

"I'd have chow mein with water chestnuts and pork—" I stop myself, but it's too late. I didn't want to remind the others of Albertine.

"I'm not hungry anymore," Jeanette announces.

"One thing I've learned," Miss E. tells us, "is that a person can get used to pretty much anything. Even hunger, thirst and lack of sleep. But we do have a great deal to be grateful for, don't we, Girl Guides?"

"You don't suppose they'll give us a day off from work, do you?" Jeanette asks Miss E.

"I don't think so," Miss E. answers brightly. "But just think how well we'll sleep tonight. Our pallets will feel as soft as Tilly's feather bed at Buckingham Palace."

"It's hard to sleep when you're hungry and thirsty," Jeanette says sadly. I know exactly what she means.

"I predict we're going to be even hungrier," Tilly says. She lifts her head toward the mess hall. There is a Japanese soldier by the door. His back is to us. He is locking the front doors with a chain and padlock.

There won't be any broomcorn or SOS today.

The pit in my stomach grows even deeper. My mouth feels drier than a desert.

It's more punishment for the boys' escape. I could be angry with the boys. It's their fault we were up all night and that we will get nothing to eat or drink today. I could also be angry with Matthew for not finding a way to say goodbye to me.

But I'm not angry.

At least, not *all* angry.

TWENTY-FOUR

Tilly thinks that since the mess hall is closed, we don't have to report for work detail.

Cathy doesn't think that's a good idea. "It isn't a day to make the Japanese soldiers more angry than they already are," she tells Tilly.

I agree with Cathy. So I come up with the plan to dust the *outside* of the mess hall. In the end, Tilly goes along with it. It doesn't make a lot of sense, because the dust will be back as soon as the winds pick up. But we still dust. At least this way we can't be accused of missing work detail. When I squat down to sweep the dust into the pan, I don't know if I'll be able to get back up.

The Japanese soldiers ignore us. They are busy searching for evidence to explain how the boys escaped. They are scouring the area near the boys' hut, looking, we think, for signs of an underground tunnel.

Tilly and I could probably get away with talking, but even that takes too much energy. If food, water and sleep are to us what gasoline is to cars, then our tanks are empty.

The armored trucks haven't returned to Weihsien. I hope it means Matthew and Benton are still on the loose. *Dear God*, I say in another silent prayer, *please keep the boys safe*. Some people think a person needs to clasp her hands to pray, or to be in a church or temple, but I don't think so. I remember something my father once told me: *Any deeply felt emotion is a prayer. The Lord will hear it.*

Those words from long ago don't fill my stomach or quench my thirst or make up for lost sleep, but somehow they make me feel less hopeless. They make it easier for me to get back up onto my feet and keep dusting.

My thoughts are interrupted by the sound of someone shouting in Japanese. The soldiers must have found a tunnel.

But when I turn my head to see what is going on, I realize that the boys didn't tunnel their way out of Weihsien. That's because one of the Japanese soldiers is holding up a small section of wooden ladder. But how could a section of ladder have helped the boys escape?

Tilly, who has also turned to see what is going on, figures out the answer before I do. "I bet the boys used a ladder to get over the electrified wall. Then afterward someone on this side chopped the ladder into pieces to hide the evidence."

Tilly and I look at each other. We are thinking the same thing: who is that someone?

The Japanese soldiers must be wondering that too, because they march off to the edge of the camp where the wells are, and where most of the boys from Matthew and Benton's hut work. About fifteen minutes later we see the soldiers marching back with three boys. They are headed to the guardhouse. "For questioning," Tilly says, and then she drops her voice. "Or worse. They'll want to talk to every one of Matthew and Benton's friends."

I almost tell Tilly that I was one of Matthew's friends. But a new thought stops me. Was Matthew ignoring me on purpose? Because if he was planning to escape, he must've known the Japanese soldiers would interrogate anyone he and Benton were close with. What did Matthew say? *Trust me—it's for the best.* Maybe—and my heart flutters a little when I think this—Matthew was trying to protect me.

When work detail finally ends, Tilly and I stumble back to the hut. We won't get any food, but I think we are both hoping we will be able to rest. Though I think that if I could choose between rest and something to eat or drink, I'd choose something to eat or drink.

The other girls are already back. Dot has burned her arm making tea in the guardhouse. She says it's because the soldiers were so snappy they made her even more nervous than usual.

Miss E. puts some black salve on Dot's arm. Miss E. looks up at all of us, but she doesn't smile. "If anyone comes to the door of the hut, I need a few of you to create a distraction," she tells us.

"What do you mean by *distraction*?" Jeanette asks.

"It means we find a way to *distract* whoever's at the door," Tilly tells her.

When Miss E. does not say, *Now, Matilda*, I know something serious is going on.

Miss E. is carrying something wrapped in a black cloth. It's hard to tell from the shape what's underneath. I can only make out one flat edge.

Miss E. takes a deep breath. "I need to do it now," she says.

"Do what?" Eunice asks.

Tilly sighs. "She means she needs to slaughter Albertine. Now."

"By yourself?" I ask Miss E.

"Yes, by myself. Lu told me how to do it. And he lent me this." Miss E. taps the black cloth lightly without showing us what is underneath.

"What if she squeals?" Tilly asks.

"Tilly!" Jeanette and I say at the same time. How can Tilly be so heartless?

Miss E. looks down at the floor, then back at us. "We thought of that," she says quietly.

"Can we say one more goodbye to Albertine?" Jeanette asks.

Miss E. shakes her head. "I don't think that's a good idea." Her eyes look sad.

Our hut has a small back door we rarely use. Now Miss E. opens the back door to reach the clearing where we've been hiding Albertine since she grew too big for keeping in the hut. We hear a small, sleepy snort. The aspirin has been working. But it sounds like Albertine is happy to have a visitor.

"What do you think Miss E. is hiding under that cloth?" I ask Tilly.

"I wish it was a gun," says Tilly. "Then she could slaughter Albertine with just one shot. It would be a painless death."

"Maybe it would make things easier if we sang," Jeanette suggests. Her eyes are wet. Which makes me wonder how people who are as dehydrated as we are can still cry. Where do the tears come from?

"I can't," I tell her.

From out back we hear Miss E.'s voice. "Keep still," she says. "Please." She isn't calling Albertine by her name. Maybe that would make it even harder for Miss E. to do what she has to do.

"Don't move!" we hear her tell Albertine. "Will you please stop moving?"

Tilly and I look at each other. It's obvious Miss E. needs help. Jeanette could never do it—she is too gentle. Tilly could. She is probably the best girl for the job. But I'm the one who loves Miss E. most, who would do anything for her.

"I'll go," I say.

TWENTY-FIVE

Miss E. is trying to get Albertine to settle on her lap. But Albertine isn't cooperating.

The piece of black cloth has fallen to the ground. I gasp when I see what is next to it. A rusty hammer with a red wooden handle.

"Gwen," Miss E. says when she sees me, "go back to the hut. Now. Albertine, sit still!"

"It might be easier if you didn't call her Albertine," I say quietly.

Miss E. is still struggling with the pig. "Gwen," she says without looking up at me, "I asked you to go back to the hut."

I avoid looking at the hammer. But I can picture the rusty hammerhead in my mind. "You can't do it alone," I tell her. "Someone has to hold Alb—" I stop myself. "The pig."

Miss E. sighs. "Fine," she says. "You may be right. I can't seem to do it by myself. If you could hold her…I mean…if you could hold the pig like this…from behind."

I grab Albertine. I hope Miss E. doesn't notice that my hands are trembling.

"Are you really going to do it with a hammer?" I ask—even though I already know the answer. Why else is there a hammer on the floor?

Miss E. swallows before she answers. "Lu told me what to do. He offered to do it himself, but I thought it would be too risky. The Japanese soldiers already have it in for Lu. The hammer is the quickest way to do it. And the quietest." Miss E. touches my arm. "Do you really think you can handle this, Gwen? You can still change your mind."

I think about Mr. Liddell starving to death in the infirmary. I think about the pit in my own belly. "I can handle this," I say, though I'm not really sure I can. I have never killed anything before. Not even a spider or an ant. I think about how, if my father found a spider in the house, he'd catch it in his cotton handkerchief and set it free outside.

I try not to wince when Miss E. picks up the hammer from the floor. "If I do it right," she says, more to herself than to me, "it should take just one blow. Lu showed me where to aim. Just up a little from between her, I mean its, eyes."

Now Miss E. is trembling. I notice it when she swings back her forearm, raising the hammer into the air. I hold the pig so tightly that I can feel her heart beating. Not for much longer, I think.

I close my eyes so I will not see the moment when the hammer hits the pig's head. But I say a silent prayer. *Let Miss E. find the spot. Thank you, Albertine.*

I hear a *crick-crack* as the hammer hits bone. The pig lets out one squeal. Just one. I open my eyes a sliver. Miss E. must have found the spot. But if she did, why is Alb— I mean, the pig—still flailing? Why are her feet still kicking? Even though my stomach is empty, I think I'm going to vomit. I want to drop the flailing pig, but I know I can't, so I don't. She struggles in my arms. Her feet are still kicking.

Miss E. lets the hammer fall to the ground. It lands with a thud.

"I did it." Miss E. sounds surprised. As if she didn't know she could slaughter a pig.

"You didn't," I say. "She's still kicking."

"Lu warned me about that. The pig's heart is still pumping. The heart doesn't know she's dead."

Then, just like that, the kicking stops. The pig's feet flop to each side. Her yellowish-brown eyes are still open, but they have a glassy, faraway look. Albertine's soul has disappeared. All that's left is her pig body.

"I need you to hold her upside down," Miss E. tells me. "So I can slit her throat."

"Slit her throat? But why? Isn't she already dead?"

"It drains the blood," Miss E. says calmly. "The meat will be tastier if we can get all the blood out. And Lu can use the blood to make blood pudding."

Miss E. takes a sharp knife out of her apron pocket. I don't ask where she got the knife. She also reaches for the tin feed bucket. "To catch the blood," she says.

This time, maybe because I know the pig is dead, I don't shut my eyes. I watch as Miss E. jams the knife into the pig's throat.

The blood—it's redder than any red I've ever seen, redder than the sunset in Weihsien, redder than the rising sun on the Japanese flag—comes gushing out like water from a hose. Miss E. holds the pail perfectly steady underneath the pig's neck. She catches nearly every drop. A little blood lands on the back of her hand. Miss E. lifts her hand to her mouth. For a second I think she's going to lick her hand clean, but then she changes her mind and lets her hand drop, wiping it on her apron.

Miss E. knows what I'm thinking. "Some people drink it raw," she says. "But I've heard it can cause worms in the brain. It's safer to let Lu make pudding from it."

Alber—the pig has only been dead ten minutes, and I already feel a little ashamed of the thoughts swirling through my head. Blood pudding, blood sausage, pork dumplings, stir-fried pork, a juicy pork chop. My mouth, always so dry and parched, begins to water.

I want to ask when exactly we will get to eat some pork.

But unlike me, Miss E.—being Miss E.—isn't thinking of herself. "If all goes well," she says quietly, "Mr. Liddell should have something to eat by this evening."

I bite my lip so hard that I taste blood.

I forgot about Mr. Liddell.

TWENTY-SIX

"A lot of things could have gone wrong," Tilly says.

We are on our way to the infirmary. Lu will be there with some roasted pork for Mr. Liddell and, of course, for us too! The thought of real food to eat makes me dizzy with anticipation.

"Instead of saying *A lot of things could have gone wrong*," Miss E. tells Tilly, "you could try saying it another way: *A lot of things went right.*"

"It's the same thing," Tilly tells Miss E.

"Not quite," Miss E. says, reaching out to brush Tilly's hair out of her eyes. "A little more positive thinking might be good for you, Matilda."

The things that went right—or that, according to Tilly, did not go wrong—are as follows: the boys have still not been caught, Miss E. was able to get Albertine's carcass to Lu, the winds have been unusually strong, so the dogs have not picked up the scent of pork, and we have prepared our musical performance for Mr. Liddell.

When we get to the infirmary, Dr. McGregor is waiting for us. He claps Miss E.'s shoulder. Lu is there too. I can't help looking at the jagged scar on his cheek. Miss E. was wrong —it doesn't make him look roguish. For a second I get a delicious whiff of roast pork. It's a good thing it's so windy and the infirmary is set apart from the huts and other buildings, or the Japanese soldiers might smell it too. If I could eat air, I swear I would open my mouth right now and take a gulp! My stomach gurgles so loudly I'm sure the others can hear it.

None of us—not even Jeanette—has mentioned Albertine's name since I helped Miss E. slaughter her. We're all too hungry to feel bad about what happened to our piglet.

Dr. McGregor stands in front of one of the gray curtains. We can hear Mr. Liddell's labored breathing. "I understand you girls have prepared a musical performance for my patient. I'd ask that you keep your performance short. Not more than ten minutes in total would be ideal. But first, why don't we all have a little something to eat?" The doctor's eyes are shining. That's when I realize he is as hungry as we are.

"Yay!" we start to cheer, but Miss E. quickly raises her finger to her mouth, and the doctor gets a worried look and says, "Shhh." They're afraid we'll draw the attention of the Japanese soldiers. I shudder when I think about how angry they would be if they knew we had managed to get something to eat.

"Your natural urge will be to eat a lot," Dr. McGregor warns us, "but you must only have small bites, and not very much at first. Your stomachs are not used to digesting large quantities, and it's been years since you've had any meat. I think we should give Mr. Liddell the honor of having the first bite. What do you think?"

We all nod, but I am wondering if the other girls are thinking the same thing as me—I can't wait much longer. And what if Mr. Liddell is so weak that it takes him forever to chew? How can I stand by and watch him eat when I am so very, very hungry?

Dr. McGregor extends his arm to open the curtain, as if we are at the theater and he is about to introduce an exciting stage act.

Mr. Liddell is sitting up but just barely. He is thinner than ever, and his skin looks gray.

"You have some visitors," Dr. McGregor tells him. "They've prepared a little entertainment for you."

"We've also got something delicious for you to eat. To help you regain your strength. Lu's wife prepared it in her own kitchen outside the camp," Miss E. tells Mr. Liddell. Lu nods when he hears his name. Miss E. does not say anything about pork. "We thought we'd join you for a little lunch before the girls present their entertainment."

Lu uncovers a cast-iron pot. Inside is a glistening mixture of little bits of meat and tiny cubes of what must be eggplant. If heaven has a smell, this, I decide, is exactly what it will smell like. Dr. McGregor hands Miss E. a pair of chopsticks. She uses them to grab hold of a little of the mixture and brings it up to Mr. Liddell's cracked, gray lips. "We'll start with just the tiniest bite." She pauses before adding, "It's pork."

I see Mr. Liddell meet Miss E.'s eyes as he opens his mouth. I can tell he understands that Albertine gave her life to feed us.

As I watch Mr. Liddell swallow, I can almost taste the salty-sweet pork.

"Delicious," Mr. Liddell says. His voice is so weak it is hard to imagine him ever sprinting in the Olympics or even standing in our hut, telling us to rotate our ankles. "Thank you," he says, and then he slumps back on his thin pillow as if having one small bite of food and saying three words has exhausted him.

"Why don't you have a second bite?" Miss E. asks him. She is already using the chopsticks to grab a little more of Lu's mixture.

Mr. Liddell shakes his head. "You eat," he says.

Lu hands around a few more pairs of chopsticks. Dr. McGregor and Miss E. let us go first. "Why don't you start with three small bites each?" the doctor suggests.

Cathy is the first of us to taste some of the mixture. She closes her eyes as she swallows.

It's the most delicious thing I've ever tasted—and not just because my stomach has been empty for over a day— and it's the first taste I've had in years of something besides broomcorn, broth with eggplant or chunks of stale bread.

I try not to eat too quickly, not swallow down the pork mix in one gulp. I let the flavor and the food's texture fill every corner of my mouth before I finally swallow. Three bites are over way too soon. I try to concentrate on what the doctor said. Our stomachs aren't ready to digest much food. Besides, it's Miss E.'s and Dr. McGregor's turns to eat.

I step away from where Lu is standing with his pan.

"What do we say to Lu?" Miss E. asks us.

"*Xiexie*," we say together, "thank you."

Lu grins and takes a small bow.

Miss E. and Dr. McGregor help themselves. Miss E. wipes her eye after she takes her first bite. I think she's remembering Albertine.

"Have they come to talk to you?" I hear the doctor ask Miss E.

"Not yet," she whispers back.

I know what they're whispering about—the Japanese soldiers are interrogating everyone who knew Matthew and Benton. They have spoken with all the boys in Matthew's hut. But my back stiffens when I realize the doctor has a point. The soldiers *will* want to talk to Miss E. too. Matthew and Benton were her students once, and she organized the rat-catching contest they won. The soldiers will know about that.

"Is one of you keeping watch out the window the way I asked you to?" Miss E. asks us.

"I am," Tilly answers. "The coast is clear."

We are each allowed to take three more bites before our performance.

I can already feel the effect of the six bites of food inside my body—it's making me stronger. But instead of feeling satisfied, I'm even hungrier than I was before. "Can we have a little more?" I ask Miss E. and Dr. McGregor.

The two of them exchange a look. "One more small bite each," Miss E. says. "There are many other prisoners who have had nothing to eat."

Her words hit me like a kick in the belly.

How could I forget about all the other people who are starving at Weihsien?

Is that what starvation does? Makes a person so selfish all she thinks about is filling her own belly?

Or would I have been like that no matter where I was, even if there wasn't a war going on and I wasn't imprisoned here?

Maybe I'm just not a very good person.

TWENTY-SEVEN

Miss E. fluffs Mr. Liddell's pillow and helps him sit up a little straighter for our performance. His face brightens when we sing our version of "Boogie Woogie Bugle Boy," complete with the arm gestures.

He was a Scottish doctor from Ed-in-burgh.
He had a friend people liked to call Miss E.
She told him thinking pos-i-tive worked as well as med-i-cine.
But then another patient turned up at his infirm-a-ry.
An Olympic med-a-list with a Scottish family tree…

Jeanette accompanies us on her paper flute.

Mr. Liddell also likes it when Cathy and Dot sing, *"Run this race, Olympic champion…"* But I can't help feeling sad during this part of the performance. Matthew thought up this version of the song. Where are Matthew and Benton now? Have the Japanese soldiers caught them? And if the boys manage not to get caught, what are the chances I'll ever see Matthew again? I am so busy thinking all this that I forget to sing along.

Tilly announces she'd like to do a solo recitation.

"How lovely, Matilda. Go ahead," Miss E. tells her.

"The Japanese are our masters. We shall not complain."

It doesn't take long for me to realize that Tilly has prepared a parody of the Twenty-Third Psalm. Knowing how religious Mr. Liddell is—he did refuse to compete on the Sabbath— I worry his feelings will be hurt.

"They maketh us to lie down on flea-infested pallets. They leadeth me to the honey pot."

How does Tilly dare to joke about the honey pot?

Miss E. must be wondering the same thing, because she grabs Tilly's wrist. "Let's not tire Mr. Liddell out, Matilda," she says, giving Tilly a sharp look.

"Nonsense," Mr. Liddell says. "Matilda's recitation is doing me good." It's the first complete sentence Mr. Liddell has uttered since we arrived. Maybe the old saying is true— laughter is the best medicine. I just never expected Mr. Liddell to laugh at a parody of the Bible. But I am learning that people don't always act the way I expect them to— that people have sides they don't always show the world. Like when I heard the fear in Miss E.'s voice when she talked about the Nanking Massacre and about not being able to protect us.

"In that case," Miss E. tells Tilly, "go ahead."

"Their goodness does not extend to Weihsien."

Miss E.'s eyes widen. Though we all know Miss E. has a good sense of humor, I don't think she likes Tilly's poem, even if it is a parody. "But God's goodness extends to Weihsien," she calls out. "It's the Lord who brought us here together for today's special event. Thank you, Matilda, for your recitation."

Tilly meets Miss E.'s eye. "I haven't finished," Tilly tells her.

Miss E. purses her lips. "Actually, you have," she says.

Mr. Liddell's eyes dart from Tilly to Miss E., then back again to Tilly. I think he is enjoying this part of the show too.

I almost forgot about Dr. McGregor, who is watching from the corner. "Miss E.," the doctor says, "I wonder if you would oblige us with a short dance number. Since rumor has it that you were part of the Birmingham Royal Ballet."

"Part of the Birmingham Royal Ballet? That sounds very fancy." Jeanette is so surprised that when her paper flute falls to the floor, she doesn't bother picking it up.

We've all heard the rumor that Miss E. danced, but I don't think we'd ever imagined that she was a professional ballerina with a royal ballet.

"I couldn't," Miss E. says. She looks down to the floor. I've never thought of Miss E. as shy, but could I have been wrong about that too?

"You couldn't?" Tilly asks. "I thought you didn't believe in *couldn't*. The word *couldn't* doesn't sound very positive to me."

It's a challenge, and we all know it.

"All right then," Miss E. says, straightening her shoulders and lengthening her neck in a way that makes it easier for me to imagine her as a professional ballerina. "Fine."

We step away from Mr. Liddell's cot to give her room. "But just a short performance. It's been many, many years. And, of course, I don't have my ballet slippers," Miss E. adds as she kicks off her boots.

Miss E. closes her eyes. I am imagining her in a pink leotard with a matching pink tulle skirt.

Miss E. starts with her feet flat on the floor and then goes up onto her toes. Why have I never noticed her elegant long neck? What she does next practically takes my breath away, it is so lovely.

Miss E. does two perfect pirouettes!

Mr. Liddell is smiling. "Wonderful," he says.

"How beautiful!" Jeanette and I say together. Everyone claps.

Without looking at any of us, Miss E. takes a small bow, then reaches for her boots. I notice that the nail on her big toe is jagged and yellow. "All right then, Girl Guides, I expect that after all this excitement Mr. Liddell needs a nap."

"Thank you ever so much for coming," Mr. Liddell tells us. "And for the performance. And the food. This has been an unforgettable morning." He rests his head on the pillow, sighing as he closes his eyes. I can see the tiny blue veins on his eyelids.

I don't understand why Mr. Liddell is so tired. He's been resting for days, and he finally got something decent to eat. It isn't as if *he* sang or recited poetry or did a double pirouette.

"Why didn't you teach us how to do ballet?" Jeanette asks Miss E. when we file out of the infirmary.

"Maybe because I like to keep a few tricks up my sleeve. Besides, you girls still have a lot to learn about geography, history, literature and mathematics," Miss E. tells her.

"Are pirouettes very hard to do?" Tilly asks.

"I believe they're the hardest part of ballet dancing," Cathy says.

"Well, Miss E. made it look easy," Jeanette tells Tilly and Cathy. "Miss E., could you teach us to do a pirouette? Then we could earn our *Dancer* badges."

"I suppose that might be possible."

If a heart could do a pirouette, that's what my heart is doing right now.

Yes, I worry the Japanese soldiers will find Matthew and Benton. Yes, our living conditions are miserable. Yes, we live in fear of our Japanese captors. And yes, I miss my parents.

But when I think about learning to do a pirouette—and earning another badge—for a moment I feel like a lucky girl.

TWENTY-EIGHT

When we get back to our hut, before I even step inside I know something's wrong.

Nothing's out of place. There's no unfamiliar sound or unfamiliar smell.

I just get a strange feeling.

And more and more, I trust my feelings. I try to pay attention to what they are telling me.

I raise my hand to signal the others.

"What's wrong?" Eunice asks.

"I'm not sure."

So I'm only half surprised when I open the door to find a Japanese soldier turning over the worn straw mattresses on our sleeping pallets. What's he looking for?

"Let me handle this," Miss E. says, pushing me aside. The roughness in her gesture is a far cry from the pirouette she did twenty minutes ago.

Then the soldier turns to look at us, and I realize it's him—the soldier who lifted Tilly and me up and let us look over the wall at the world outside Weihsien.

"It's our friend," I tell Miss E. As soon as I say the words, I realize how strange it feels to call a Japanese soldier *our friend*. Only in this case, it's true.

Miss E.'s shoulders relax. She's figured out which soldier I mean. "*Konnichiwa*," she says, bowing to him. But it's a very different bow from the one she took in the infirmary. This time she bows from the waist, and there isn't even a quarter ounce of pride in it. It's the bow we have to give to every Japanese soldier, the bow that signals we understand the Imperial Army's power over us, that we must obey its soldiers' every command.

The Japanese soldier lets the mattress he was holding drop back onto the wooden pallet. Dust particles dance in the air, then disappear. I don't think he found what he was looking for. Now he gestures for Miss E. to follow him outside, behind the hut. We trail after her. He could tell us not to, but he doesn't. I gulp when I realize he's bringing Miss E. to the exact spot where I watched her kill Albertine. I lick the corner of my mouth. The sweet taste of pork is still on my lips.

He points at something on the ground and grunts. It's a rusty brown spot. Dried pig's blood. I bring my hand to my mouth. I thought we got rid of all the evidence.

"*Souji!*" the soldier says. It's an order, though I have no idea what *souji* means.

Miss E. does. "Yes," she tells him. "Right away. Thank you. Thank you very much. *Arigatou*." Miss E. turns to us. "See if you can find a bucket and any water at all. Even waste water. Right away, Girl Guides! If there's no waste water, we'll use spit instead."

Souji must mean "clean it up." Instead of punishing us, this soldier is trying to protect us. I'm so relieved I could cry.

It's not hard to find a bucket outside the latrine, but there's no water, not even waste water. So we use spit. Jeanette's eyes fill with tears as we spit over the rusty spot. She is remembering Albertine. But there isn't time to worry about Jeanette. The Japanese soldier has disappeared, but who knows when he—or another, less kind soldier— will be back.

"It goes to show that not all the Japanese soldiers are monsters," Jeanette says when we are finished, and there is no trace left of pig's blood. "That soldier didn't have to be kind to us—but he was."

"He's the same one who lifted us up so we could see over the wall," I say.

"I told you he was kind," Jeanette says.

"It doesn't mean we can trust him," Tilly says.

It's not that I don't expect Tilly to say something negative, because I do. That's Tilly. It's just that I don't expect her to say something negative about *this* soldier. He put himself at risk by letting us look outside Weihsien and now by pointing out the spot of pig's blood on the ground and warning us to clean it up. If another soldier found out any of this, our new friend could be accused of treason.

Maybe it's the feeling of a little food in my belly after so long that gives me energy to argue. "Do you think, Tilly, that for once, just once, you could try not to be so negative?" My voice comes out sounding shriller than I want it to. And I'm not finished. "What would be so terrible about trusting someone kind?"

Tilly's eyes widen. I think it's because in all the years we've been friends, I've never spoken back to her.

I know Tilly is about to answer me. I expect her to raise her voice the way I just did. But when she speaks, her voice is so calm it's eerie. "You know what's wrong with you, Gwen? You've swallowed Miss E.'s philosophy whole, without giving it time to digest in your brain. Don't you see what she's been doing all these years? She wants us to see the world the way she wants it to be—not the way it really is."

TWENTY-NINE

A group of coolies is working on the electrified stone wall that separates us from the outside world. Some are hauling gray boulders in wheelbarrows; others are passing boulders to coolies who are perched on ladders by the wall. All of their faces are dripping with sweat, and there are dark sweat stains under their armpits. Two Japanese soldiers stand near the bottom of the ladders, their arms crossed over their chests, supervising and occasionally barking out orders.

They are making the wall a full foot higher, and soon the world of Weihsien will get even darker.

It's because of Matthew and Benton. The Japanese want to make sure there will be no more escapes from Weihsien. Miss E. explained to us that something called *saving face* means a lot to the Japanese. If two boys are able to elude the Imperial Army, the Japanese lose face. Meaning they look like fools. So everything the Japanese have done since the boys escaped—taking away our food and waking us up for extra roll calls, interrogating everyone who knew the boys and, now, extending the wall—is a way of saving face.

Pride is a strange thing. It's all right to be proud of your accomplishments, as long as you don't get too conceited. When I look at the rows of badges on my uniform, especially the one that says *Artist*, I feel proud. That kind of pride makes a person want to do more great things. For example, I would like to earn more badges. I would like my uniform to be so covered in badges it would be hard to see the blue cloth underneath!

But too much pride can be dangerous. I remember how, during one of his sermons, my father warned that too much pride can prevent us from knowing Him, meaning the Good Lord.

Perhaps the Japanese care too much about saving face. Maybe they should think about their day-to-day behavior and how they treat us. But then I remind myself that not all of the Japanese are like that. Not the soldier who lifted us up and alerted us to the bloodstains on the ground. I don't care what Tilly says—that Japanese soldier is our friend.

We are headed to morning roll call. Miss E. doesn't have to tell us *not* to stare at the coolies working on the wall. We have learned to make ourselves invisible. We can't risk upsetting the Japanese, especially when they are still smarting after the boys' escape.

Because I don't know where else to look, I look at my feet. The tip of my big right toe is hanging over the sole of my shoe. Even if we are not getting enough to eat or drink, our bodies are still growing. That thought makes me glad. We may be prisoners—*sojourners*—but our captors cannot control everything about us.

Because I am looking at my big toe I don't see the two Japanese soldiers marching in our direction. But Jeanette sees them, and she makes a hiccupping sound.

At first I think the soldiers are on their way to join the pair supervising the coolies' work. But when one stops in front of us and raises his hand in the air, his palm outstretched, I realize I'm wrong. I also know from the stony look on this soldier's face that something bad is about to happen.

"*Ohayo gozaimasu*," Miss E. says brightly. I have never admired Miss E. as much as I admire her right now. If she is afraid of the Japanese soldier, she does not let it show.

The soldier speaks to Miss E. in rapid-fire Japanese. Each word sounds as harsh and deadly as a bullet.

"I'm afraid I don't understand what you're saying," Miss E. tells the soldier, looking right at him as she speaks. "Though my Japanese is coming along, I still have a long way to go. And you do speak very quickly."

The soldier reaches inside his jacket and takes a piece of paper from his pocket. The paper is folded into four.

The soldier wants Miss E. to look at what's on the paper. "I'll need my glasses," she tells him, using her thumbs and index fingers to make a circle over each of her eyes.

When the soldier grunts, Miss E. takes her glasses out of her apron.

Though I know I shouldn't move from my spot and draw attention to myself, I lean slightly over so I can peek at the paper too. I have to hold in a gasp when I see that it's a kind of map—a lot like the map I drew for Matthew in the dirt.

But why does the soldier suspect Miss E. knows something about this map?

It's only when the soldier turns the paper over that I understand why he was barking at Miss E. There's a multiplication table on the other side of the paper. As soon as I see the neatly written numbers and the carefully drawn lines separating the columns, I recognize Miss E.'s handwriting.

The soldier doesn't wait for Miss E. to say something. He grabs hold of her collar and pulls her toward him—and away from us.

"Miss—" Cathy starts to say.

Miss E.'s lips twitch. She wants to tell us something. But she doesn't use words. Instead she purses her lips and blows us a kiss.

It's Miss E.'s turn to be taken for interrogation. And there is nothing we can do to help her. But I think we all understand there was a message in that kiss she blew us.

We are Girl Guides. Miss E. expects us to hold our heads high and go to roll call.

THIRTY

If Miss E. had nothing to do with the boys' escape, why is she being held so long in the Imperial Army's office?

Roll call is over. Work detail is done. Dot, who was in the guardhouse making tea for the Japanese officers, tried to get news about Miss E., but she couldn't find out anything.

The others are content to wait in the hut, but Tilly and I can't stand not knowing. So we decide to sneak to the center of the camp, where we find a shady spot across from the Imperial Army's office. Made of red brick, it's one of the only well-maintained buildings in this part of the camp. The windows are clean, and there's not a single broken pane. As usual, the shades are down, making it impossible to see what goes on inside.

"Why would they keep an innocent person so long?" I ask Tilly.

"Because they can," she says simply. "Besides, why are you so sure she's innocent?"

"Because she's Miss E.," I tell her. "She would never do anything wrong."

Tilly looks at me and shakes her head. "She might do something wrong—if she thought it could lead to something right."

I don't know what to say to that. How can something wrong lead to something right? I hate when Tilly talks in riddles.

"How do you think the boys got hold of a ladder?" she asks.

"I…uh…I don't know. Miss E. doesn't own a ladder."

"No," Tilly says, "of course not. But the Imperial Army does, and I'm sure the coolies have ladders too."

"What does that have to do with Miss E.? She isn't in the army, and she isn't a coolie."

Tilly sighs. She thinks she is a lot smarter than me—and maybe she is. Could Miss E. really have helped the boys to escape? "Miss E. has many friends" is all Tilly will say.

Tilly suddenly grabs hold of my hand, clutching it so hard her fingernails dig into my wrist. The door to the office is opening. Two Japanese soldiers march out, heads held high. Miss E. is propped up between them. Each soldier is holding one of her elbows. Thank God Miss E. seems to be all right. We are too far away to make out her expression. Her hair looks mussed up, but her spine is as straight as ever.

She is the bravest person I have ever known. I can't imagine what it would feel like to be interrogated by Japanese soldiers for almost three hours.

I move to get up. I need to go to Miss E. But Tilly stops me. "It isn't safe," she whispers. I know she's right. The Japanese soldiers will want to know what we are doing here, so far from our hut.

Someone else comes out of the office. I think Tilly is as surprised as I am to see it is the camp commander himself. I tremble when I see him. He is a large man in every way—nearly as tall, and with a trunk as thick, as a banyan tree. He says something in loud Japanese, and the soldiers who have Miss E. between them turn to look at him, then click the heels of their boots.

Miss E. turns too. The commander is speaking to her. His voice booms so much we hear its echo in our hiding spot. We don't understand what he is saying. But we recognize his tone—angry, cruel and mocking. The commander stretches out his arm and extends an upturned palm toward Miss E. He is ordering her to give him something. Now!

When Miss E.'s shoulders slump, I bite my lip.

And when Miss E. reaches into her apron pocket, I realize what the commander wants. Miss E.'s reading glasses. But why? He must have his own pair. After all, he's the camp commander!

Miss E. holds on to the glasses for a few seconds longer than seems necessary. The commander barks again, and she lays the reading glasses in his palm. Poor Miss E. How will she be able to read without her glasses?

Nothing could prepare me for what happens next. I'll never forget it. Not if I live to be a hundred.

The commander tosses Miss E.'s glasses to the ground in front of him. Then he lifts one foot, letting it hover just over the glasses. Though we are too far away to hear, I wince as I imagine the sound of his shiny black boot stomping down hard on Miss E.'s glasses, and the shattered glass flying up into the air and tinkling as it hits the ground.

The commander laughs, and then, as if they were waiting for instructions, the soldiers laugh too.

Only one small thing brings me comfort. Miss E. straightens her shoulders.

"How will she be able to read?" I whisper to Tilly. "How will she be able to give us lessons?"

"Don't you see? That's why he did it." Tilly spits out the words. "So she won't be able to rea—" Tilly doesn't finish her sentence. She has raised her eyes to signal that someone is nearby. We could get into all sorts of trouble if anyone finds us here.

My body tenses when I realize that it's another Japanese soldier. This one must have been watching the scene too.

Tilly tugs on my hand. "Let's go," she hisses as she hunches down, preparing to disappear into the shadows and take me with her.

The bushy eyebrows tell me who it is. Our friend. My friend. But I know it would be risky to speak to him now or acknowledge him in any way. So I follow Tilly back to our hut. She is as quick and quiet as a cat.

"Guides!" Miss E. calls when, a few minutes later, she walks into our hut. I hear something forced in her voice. I wonder if it's possible that for all these years Miss E. has just been pretending to be cheerful, the way I know she is pretending now.

"Miss E.!" We all rush to her, grabbing hold of her at the same time. Her shoulder bones feel as brittle as sticks.

"Don't squeeze me too hard," she says. "Or I might break."

Even if it's a joke, Miss E.'s words worry me. What would happen to us if Miss E. broke?

THIRTY-ONE

It's Jeanette who insists that Miss E. take a nap. "I could read to you," Jeanette says once Miss E. is settled on the sleeping pallet. "From the Bible."

"I'd like that," Miss E. says, closing her eyes.

Dot gets Miss E.'s Bible from the trunk. The Bible has a lovely silk ribbon that marks the page Miss E. was on. Dot hands the Bible to Jeanette, who is sitting on the edge of the mattress. Jeanette opens to the page where the silk ribbon is.

"*Now the Phil...*" Jeanette has trouble with the word.

"Philistines, dear," Miss E. says, without opening her eyes.

"*Phil i stines,*" Jeanette continues, "*gathered together their armies to battle, and were gathered together at Shochoh.*" She is reading the story of David and Goliath. I know because I've always loved that story. "*They pitched between*

Shochoh and Azekah, in Ephesdamm…"—Jeanette stumbles over the words.

"Here, let me help," Miss E. says. Jeanette leans closer to Miss E., who sits up a little and reaches into her apron pocket. When she does, I see her swallow hard. I know why. She has remembered about her glasses.

Miss E. reaches for the Bible and peers into it. Then she brings it even closer to her face, so close the yellowed pages almost touch her nose. "I can't see a thing," she mutters to herself.

"Where are your glasses?" Cathy asks Miss E.

Miss E. laughs. "My glasses?" she says. "Those pesky things. I've gone and lost them." Miss E. laughs again. Underneath the laugh, I hear what sounds like a sob. And I don't think I imagined it.

"In that case, we'll help you look for them," Jeanette offers. "Right, girls?"

"Of course we will," the other girls say. But Tilly and I exchange a look. We don't know what to answer.

"There's no point looking," Miss E. tells Jeanette. "I'm quite sure they're gone."

"But how will you manage without glasses?" Jeanette asks. "I heard you say you can't read a single word without them. And we all know how much you love to read."

"I'll manage," Miss E. tells her. "There are worse things in the world than losing a silly pair of reading glasses." Though Miss E.'s voice sounds peppy, there is something hollow in her tone. As if, for once, she really is thinking about worse things in the world. I feel sorry for Miss E.—and also afraid. What if Miss E. really does break? What if she can't keep pretending to be cheerful? Then what will happen to us?

"If you don't mind," Miss E. tells Jeanette, "I really could use a little nap. Without reading. We'll try again tomorrow when the light is better in here. Then I won't miss my glasses one bit." I know that isn't true. Better light won't make a difference. "A little quiet time will do me good," Miss E. continues. "Why don't you girls go and get some fresh air?"

I don't say what I'm thinking. That between the mugginess, the dust and how close we are to the latrines, there's nothing fresh about the air at Weihsien.

But because Miss E. asked us, we head outside and sit on the stoop.

"The commander stomped on Miss E.'s glasses," I tell Jeanette and the other girls. I don't know why I tell them, but I don't regret it. Not even when Jeanette's eyes get big.

"Why would he do something like that?" she asks.

"Because he can." The second the words are out of my mouth, I realize that not too long ago Tilly said the same thing to me. I never imagined that one day I would sound like Tilly.

"We should find a way to turn it into a game," Jeanette says.

"Turn what into a game?" Tilly asks her.

Jeanette squeezes each of our hands. "A game of Miss E. not having her glasses. It could be like blindman's bluff. I've always loved that game."

Maybe it's the innocence in Jeanette's voice when she says *I've always loved that game*. Maybe it's the hopefulness in the way she is squeezing my hand.

Or maybe it's both.

Whatever it is, it makes my blood begin to boil.

"Can't you just shut up?" I say, shaking my hand loose so violently that Jeanette falls backward to the ground.

"Stop it!" Cathy says, but I don't pay any attention.

Even Tilly is shocked by what I've done. She starts to say my name, but I cut her off. I'm not finished. And I don't care that Jeanette is struggling to get up. "You can't make a game of what's happened to Miss E.'s glasses! That's as stupid as making a game of what's going on inside this awful place. We're not sojourners, Jeanette. We're prisoners. And the Japs aren't happy simply starving us to death. They want to break our spirits."

Jeanette has gotten up, but she moves away from me— as if she's afraid I might smack her. "Well then," she says, "we shouldn't let them."

"Don't you see, you idiot, there's nothing we can do to stop them. Nothing!"

I don't know what comes over me then. A tsunami of rage I've never felt before and did not know I had inside me. Maybe it's the way Jeanette moved away from me that spurs me on. I make a fist and shake it in Jeanette's face. So many thoughts are going through my head. Albertine in her bonnet. My parents abandoning me in Chefoo. Matthew pretending not to know me. But mostly Jeanette and how she thinks we can make a game of Miss E.'s blindness. Blindman's bluff. Jeanette's the blind one. She's the one who's being bluffed. As for me, I'm sick and tired of being bluffed, of being blind.

In my thirteen years on planet Earth, I have never hit another person. I've never even thought of hitting someone. But now I swear it's like I can't stop myself any more than I could stop a tsunami.

I feel my knuckles make contact with the side of Jeanette's face. I feel warm liquid. Is it tears—or blood? I don't know, but I'm still angry. I'm even angrier.

I can't stop myself.

Cathy and Dot pull me off Jeanette. Tilly tells me to calm down and that I should be ashamed of myself.

Only I'm not ashamed of myself.

That comes later.

Then the Japanese soldier—the one who is my friend— is suddenly there, hurrying up the gravel path toward our hut. His eyes are full of sadness and understanding.

He gestures that he has something to show us. He uncurls his hand.

It's a pair of reading glasses.

"Where did you get those?" Dot asks.

He shrugs. He doesn't understand Dot's question.

But in Weihsien, those glasses come from the same place as everything else, whether it's shoes, boots, pants or an old tattered shirt. Those glasses must have belonged to a prisoner who died here.

THIRTY-TWO

I don't usually cry, but now I can't stop. In the same way I couldn't stop myself from getting angry before. Giant, noisy sobs that make my whole body heave.

I'm crying because I'm sorry I hit Jeanette and shouted at her and called her an idiot. I'm also crying because of the reading glasses. *See!* I want to tell Tilly! *He is our friend.* But I am crying too hard to make words.

Jeanette is crying too and stroking her cheek. The skin is red and swollen, but I don't see blood. Those must have been tears I felt before.

"I'm sorry," I sputter. "I'm really, really sorry." I want to explain that something terrible came over me, but I can't because I can't explain it to myself.

Cathy examines Jeanette's face. Tilly has squeezed herself between Jeanette and me, as if she thinks she might have to block me from hitting Jeanette again. "I'm sorry," I say, this time to Tilly's back. "Please forgive me."

"I don't know if I can forgive you." Jeanette half sobs the words. "But I'll try. Why do you think she went crazy like that?" she asks Tilly. She means me, of course.

I don't expect Tilly to have an answer. I don't have it myself. And though Tilly doesn't usually go around quoting Miss E. the way I do, she does that now. And what she says makes sense. "Remember what Miss E. says: *Anger is sadness turned inside out.*"

I look down at my worn Girl Guide uniform. I'd never wear it inside out because the stitching would show. The stitching holds my uniform together. Without the inside there'd be no outside. Is it the same with anger and sadness?

Because right now there's nothing left of the white-hot anger I felt when I hit Jeanette. All that's left is a sadness so deep I think I may never be able to climb out of it.

"The glasses," Jeanette says. "We have to bring them to Miss E. To see if they're a good fit for her eyes."

I follow the others back inside our hut. Miss E. is wiping the sleep from her eyes. Does that mean she slept through my outburst? I pray the other girls won't tell her what I did. I know it's wrong to waste a prayer on a selfish thought, but I can't help it. What would Miss E. think of me if she knew that I hit Jeanette, who is the gentlest and kindest of all of us? Would Miss E. ever look at me in the same way?

For a split second I catch Jeanette's eye. I can't look at her cheek. *Please don't tell*, I say, mouthing the words.

Jeanette meets my gaze. Her expression is blank, but then she nods. She isn't going to tell on me.

I don't know if I'd have done the same if she'd hit me.

We go to stand by the pallet where Miss E. is still resting. The soldier hands the glasses to Miss E. Like the ones the commander destroyed, these glasses have wire rims.

"Oh my!" Miss E. says. "Reading glasses. How very, very kind of you. I'm so moved I don't know what to say…"

When she puts the reading glasses on, they slip down to the tip of her nose. The soldier unhooks the glasses from behind Miss E.'s ears, then bends the wire arms. He hands the glasses back to Miss E. They fit better now.

"Here," Jeanette says, opening the Bible to the page Miss E. couldn't read before. "Can you make out the words?"

We wait for Miss E.'s verdict.

"They're a little blurry," she says, "but yes." Miss E. turns to the soldier. "*Arigatou gozaimasu.*"

Then the soldier does something I've never seen a Japanese soldier do before. He bows down low—to Miss E.

I wish the day could end right there. On this hopeful note. That's where I would end it if I was the one telling the story. But not all days go like that.

The soldier is leaving when we hear men's voices outside the hut. They are speaking Japanese, but also some English.

Two Japanese soldiers burst into the hut. Dr. McGregor is with them.

Miss E. removes the glasses and stuffs them into her apron pocket. I hope the soldiers don't notice.

One soldier shouts something when he sees our visitor. The other soldier grabs hold of our friend. That's when I realize I don't even know the man's name. Why didn't I ever think to ask him when he lifted me and Tilly above the stone wall or when he warned us about the bloodstains behind the hut?

"What's going on?" Miss E. asks Dr. McGregor.

The doctor looks down at the floor, then back up at Miss E. "It's Mr. Liddell," he says. "He passed."

Miss E. crumbles. There's no other word to describe it. Her chin sags to her chest, and her shoulders shake. It's the first time I've ever seen someone cry without making a sound.

I want to comfort her, but I know I can't. Not with the Japanese soldiers standing so close.

I don't need to understand Japanese to know that now the two soldiers are interrogating our friend. They want to know what he's doing in our hut. He points to the empty honey pot. Maybe he's telling them he has come for a spot inspection.

I can tell from their angry voices that they do not believe him.

One of the soldiers lunges toward Miss E. "Don't hurt—" I start to say, but Miss E. shoots me a warning look and I stop myself.

But this soldier isn't trying to hurt her. He gestures at her apron. He must have noticed that she hid something there before. He wants her to show him what it is.

Miss E.'s face turns whiter than snow.

She can't turn this into a game.

She takes out the reading glasses.

Our friend doesn't resist when the other two Japanese soldiers drag him out of the hut.

No one could call our friend a sojourner.

Like us, he's been taken prisoner.

THIRTY-THREE

Our friend's name is Corporal Hashimoto. Dr. McGregor tells Miss E., who tells us. She also tells us that Corporal Hashimoto is being held in a small cell in the guardhouse.

I am waiting for Miss E. to say we should think positive thoughts, or for her to distract us with a lesson or a game, but she doesn't. That scares me as much as the idea that Corporal Hashimoto will be severely punished, maybe even killed, for bringing Miss E. those eyeglasses. By doing so, he has proven himself to be a traitor to the Imperial Japanese Army. For the Japanese, there is no greater crime.

Tilly thinks Miss E. is depressed. Not only because she must feel responsible for Corporal Hashimoto's situation, but also because she is mourning Mr. Liddell. "I think she was in love with him," Tilly says. "Mr. Liddell wasn't good-looking, but he was an Olympic champion."

"That's impossible. I heard Mr. Liddell had a wife," Jeanette chimes in.

"So what? Miss E. could still have been in love with him. And him with her," Tilly says.

"A person doesn't have to be in love with another person to be sorry that they're gone," I say. I am thinking about Matthew. I am too young to be in love, but I miss everything about him—his dark eyes, his smile...even the way he sometimes laughed at me. I miss that most of all.

I also think about the time I overheard Miss E. and Mr. Liddell chatting behind the mess hall. I wondered then if they had planned to meet up. I remember how they were discussing the awful things the Imperial Japanese Army did in Nanking. Which makes me worry all over again about Corporal Hashimoto.

Jeanette is worried about him too. "You don't really think they'd hurt him, do you?" she asks Tilly. Even though I apologized, Jeanette has not spoken to me directly since the incident. I don't blame her. Her cheek is less swollen, but now it's got a bluish-yellow sheen. My stomach turns sour with guilt every time I see it.

"Who do you mean by *him*?" Tilly asks her.

"Corporal Hashimoto."

Tilly sighs. "Of course they will hurt him. That's what the Imperial Japanese Army does best. Hurt people. It's a way to show their power and create fear. People who are afraid cause less trouble. They don't try to escape."

I nearly mention Nanking—but then I change my mind. "In that case," I say instead, "we have to find a way to help Corporal Hashimoto."

"What are you planning?" Jeanette asks. I'm glad she's finally speaking to me. Except then she adds, "Maybe you think it might help to sock a Japanese soldier in the face."

"I said I was sorry," I tell her.

"There isn't anything we can do to help Corporal Hashimoto," Tilly says. "We're just a bunch of girls. If you ask me, they'll probably kill him. Of course, they'll torture him first. Then they'll behead him and display his severed head on a pole. To make a lesson of him to the other soldiers. To show them what happens if they are the least bit kind to any of us."

Tilly's words send a chill up and down my spine. I hadn't thought about the Imperial Japanese Army wanting to use Corporal Hashimoto for a lesson, but what Tilly said makes perfect sense. Yet there is one part of what she said that I disagree with.

"We're not just a bunch of girls," I remind Tilly. "We're Girl Guides."

"Well then, what's your plan?" Tilly asks.

"I don't have one yet."

"That isn't very good news for Corporal Hashimoto," Tilly points out.

Jeanette has a plan, though it has nothing to do with Corporal Hashimoto. She wants to make an infusion for Miss E. to drink that might improve her mood.

The three of us go to the infirmary to see if Dr. McGregor can help us. He recommends something called *fog tea*. It's made from an herb grown in eastern China, and he happens to have a small sample in his supply cabinet. "It's sometimes used to treat melancholy," the doctor tells us. "There's no harm in letting Miss E. have a cup."

It's when the doctor uses the word *harm* that I begin to hatch a plan. I need to find a way to prevent Corporal Hashimoto from being harmed. There's no harm in fog tea. But there are other herbs that can cause harm.

It was Miss E. who taught us about wolfsbane.

A pretty blue flower that is part of the buttercup family, wolfsbane doesn't look poisonous. Neither does the snow-white amanita mushroom, which, when eaten raw, is the most lethal mushroom.

"Wolfsbane is also known as monkshood," Miss E. told us during one of our biology lessons. "My uncle Edward, the chemist—I told you how he had a mustache a little like a rat's—well, he taught me that. Uncle Edward was very interested in herbal cures, and, for that matter, in herbal poisons too. It's called wolfsbane because it was believed to ward off werewolves. Isn't that fascinating, Girl Guides? Wolfsbane slows the pulse, acting like a sedative. There's loads of it around Weihsien. Why, I've seen bunches of it growing behind the watchtower. But be sure never to ingest wolfsbane, because that lovely blue flower can kill a grown man in no time."

I decide not to involve Tilly or Jeanette in my plan. Not because I couldn't use their help, but because I know that any prisoner caught trying to poison a Japanese soldier will be executed on the spot. I am willing to risk my own life, but not my friends' lives. Not that I want to die.

From what I can tell there is only one soldier in the guardhouse keeping watch over Corporal Hashimoto. My plan is not to kill the soldier who is keeping guard— only to sedate him long enough for Corporal Hashimoto to escape from Weihsien. When I imagine Corporal Hashimoto's escape, I see him meeting up with Matthew and Benton—and then the three of them join forces and find a way to release all of us from captivity here in Weihsien.

But there's no point in thinking about those things now.

The first thing I have to do is find some wolfsbane.

The clump of pretty blue flowers is exactly where Miss E. said it would be. Behind the watchtower. The blue petals would be perfect for pressing inside a book and then, when they were dry, using to decorate a greeting card.

Because I don't know how much wolfsbane I need to sedate a grown man, I pick as much as I can. The stalks leave a trail of green markings on my fingers. I'm careful not to touch my lips. Who knows what could happen to me if I accidentally swallowed some wolfsbane.

Would I die on the spot?

I don't want to die.

I want to live to be a grown-up.

I want to be like Miss E. and Corporal Hashimoto.

I want to do good turns—and not only to earn more badges.

But what if a person has to do a terrible, evil thing in order to do a good turn?

THIRTY-FOUR

According to Dot, the Japanese soldiers have a lot of rules when it comes to tea. They only drink green tea, and the water has to be the perfect temperature. Dot boils the water in a pot, but then she has to let it cool for exactly three minutes before pouring it over the tea leaves. The tea also has to be the perfect color. Dot calls it turtle green.

We're all thinking about tea this afternoon.

Jeanette has made a fog-tea infusion for Miss E. Dot, the tea expert in our hut, helps serve it to Miss E. Dot also helps Jeanette prop Miss E. up on the sleeping pallet so she can take small sips. "How do you like the taste?" I hear the girls ask her.

"It's...interesting," Miss E. answers, which is how I know it must taste awful. But Miss E. would never say so.

"Dot, since you're helping Jeanette look after Miss E., I was wondering if it would help if I took over your work detail at the guardhouse," I say. "You've told us so much about preparing the green tea for the Japanese soldiers, I'm sure I could do it for you. Turtle green and all. Then you could stay here and help Jeanette."

"I'd be happy to get a break from the guardhouse," Dot says. "Are you sure you don't mind filling in?"

"It's the least I can do. For you...and for Jeanette."

Jeanette turns to look at me. Because I want her to think I'm doing Dot and her a favor, and not planning an evil deed, I add, "I was also thinking that if I took over Dot's work detail and she was around to help you, well, you might feel more like forgiving me for..." I am about to say *what happened*, but then I decide it's better to acknowledge what I did. "For smacking you."

"I *have* forgiven you," Jeanette says.

I'm so glad to hear this that for a minute I forget all about my plan. But then I remember. "Okay then," I say to Jeanette and Dot, "you two keep looking after Miss E. Dot, I'll take over at the guardhouse. You don't even need to come and check on me." I look into Dot's eyes when I say this so she'll understand that she shouldn't come anywhere near the guardhouse. If anyone suspects a soldier has been poisoned, I have to be the one to take the blame.

I don't believe in premonitions. At least, I've never had one. But on my way to the guardhouse, I have the strangest experience.

It starts with the smell of lavender. And then I see her— my mother. She looks the way she always did. Her hair piled on top of her head in a neat bun. She reaches out to squeeze my hand. When I look into her eyes, I can tell that she has come to warn me about something.

Does she know about the wolfsbane in my pocket?

Is that why she's come?

I rub my eyes. Mother can't be in Weihsien. She's at the other end of China with my father, doing missionary work. But even when I rub my eyes, she doesn't go away. I take a few steps closer. Maybe it really is her.

"Mother!" I call out as I open my arms and rush to her.

"Don't," she tells me. "Don't."

And then, just like that, she's gone.

Where did she go? And what was she trying to tell me?

Don't what? Don't try to poison the Japanese soldier who is guarding Corporal Hashimoto?

I think about Corporal Hashimoto and all the good turns he did for us. Now I think of something else. Was it Corporal Hashimoto who gave the boys the ladder they used to climb the wall and escape Weihsien? And are the other Japanese soldiers wondering that too?

I don't have a choice. If I don't try to save Corporal Hashimoto, who will? I have to do something.

I pat my pocket where the wolfsbane is. That helps me stay focused on what I need to do.

The guardhouse is eerily quiet. No Japanese soldier is standing guard outside. There's no soldier in the front room. I take a deep breath and walk in. The tea things are exactly where Dot said they'd be. There is water in a pot on the stove. I light the burner.

There's a metal canister with loose tea leaves in it on a shelf by the stove. I look over both of my shoulders to make sure I'm still alone. My heart thumps in my chest. Do it now, I tell myself. *Don't*, I hear the woman with my mother's face say.

That woman was just part of my imagination. Maybe the wolfsbane that stained my fingers got into my blood system and is causing a mild hallucination.

I reach into my pocket and add some of the blue flowers to the tea leaves. Not too many, not too few. I want to call out and tell Corporal Hashimoto that it's me, that I'm here to rescue him, but I know I can't draw attention to myself—or to him.

I concentrate on preparing the tea. I pour the water over the leaves. My hands shake a little, but that could be because the pot is heavier than I expected, and I don't want to burn myself the way Dot did. I pour the water into a small, squat porcelain teapot.

I worried the wolfsbane might have an odor, but it doesn't. Will the tea turn turtle green or might it have a bluish tint? If it does, my plan could fail, and the Japanese soldiers will know what I'm planning.

Someone's at the door. When I turn and look to see who it is, I nearly gasp.

It's the Japanese soldier whose dog had the piece of glass in its front paw. The same soldier that Tilly said she saw kicking his dog.

If he recognizes me, he doesn't show it.

The three minutes is nearly up. It's time for me to serve the tea.

I know I can't look at the soldier. I focus on what's inside the porcelain teapot. Turtle green, I think to myself, please be turtle green. It is. Perfectly turtle green without any blue at all.

The Japanese soldier grunts as he approaches me. Four porcelain cups are lined up on the counter. They don't have handles like my mother's teacups do. They must be very hot to hold. What if the soldier burns his hands?

That thought nearly makes me laugh out loud. Why am I worrying about the soldier burning his hands when I am about to poison him?

The soldier taps his ears, then slowly brings his hands down to his shoulders. He juts out his chin as if he is asking me something.

"I don't understand," I start to say, but then I realize what it is. His gesture is meant to indicate Dot's long hair. He wants to know why she isn't here, making him his tea.

I pat my belly. "She has a tummy ache," I say. "Ow."

I think he understands because he nods, then lifts his chin toward the row of teacups. He wants his tea.

I reach for the teapot, letting it hover over the first teacup. I didn't need to worry so much about the color of the tea because the inside of the cup is dark brown. The tea has the lovely earthy fragrance of green tea.

The soldier doesn't move. He is waiting for me to hand him his cup. I bow low to show that I understand. So there is a chance that my fingers will get burned.

I don't want to kill this soldier—even if he has mistreated his dog. I only want to conk him out long enough for me to help Corporal Hashimoto escape from his holding cell. But there's a chance that my wolfsbane infusion will be fatal.

I take a deep breath. The teacup is even hotter than I expected. So hot I can't grip it with all my fingers. "Oh no," I say as I let go of the cup and it crashes to the floor, shattering into a thousand pieces. There is green tea with wolfsbane in it everywhere.

"I'm sorry," I stammer, reaching for a cleaning rag I spotted by the stove and bending down to mop up the mess.

The soldier steps right over the porcelain shards. I hear them crunch under the weight of his black boots. He opens the door to the adjoining room, which must be the holding cell.

From my spot on the floor I can see everything. The holding cell is about the size of the closet in our bedroom at the boarding school in Chefoo.

I see signs of a scuffle. A pail lying on its side. A military jacket with a torn sleeve. One glistening black boot.

At first I think the holding cell is empty.

But then my eyes land on a crumpled figure at the back of the cell. I see the matching black boot at the end of a leg in khaki-colored pants. There is something strange about the position of the leg, the way it is flung to one side at a right angle. No person would ever lie down in such an uncomfortable way.

That is not Corporal Hashimoto, I tell myself. Not any more than the pig with its hammered-in skull and slit throat was Albertine. That is only Corporal Hashimoto's body.

I let out one dry sob. The Japanese soldier turns to look at me. He points to the mess on the floor, and I get back to my cleaning.

THIRTY-FIVE

"What's going on?" Miss E. asks me. She is outside our hut. The color is coming back to her face.

"Are you feeling better?" When I ask the question I realize I'm doing what Miss E. does: changing the subject to avoid a difficult discussion.

"Jeanette's fog tea did the trick," Miss E. says. "Of course, I'm sad—we're all sad about Mr. Liddell's passing. But he would want us to carry on and stay hopeful. That performance you girls did for him—I know he was deeply moved by it. I wanted to thank all of you for being so wonderful—always. Now if you could tell me, Gwen, what's going on? Have you seen Corporal Hashimoto? You were over at the guardhouse preparing tea, weren't you?"

Part of me wants to tell Miss E. everything. How I tried to poison the soldier, how at the last second the teacup slipped out of my hand and how I saw Corporal Hashimoto's corpse on the floor.

"Tell me everything, Gwen." The way Miss E. says it—insistent yet gentle—makes me wonder if she can read my thoughts. Does she know how torn apart I am inside?

Another part of me says, *No, don't tell Miss E. everything.* Miss E. doesn't need to know that Corporal Hashimoto is dead.

There are chinks in Miss E.'s armor. She is not always 100 percent brave, positive, cheerful and hopeful. That's just what she wants us to think. I heard the fear in her voice when she was talking about the Battle of Nanking. And I saw the sadness in her eyes when she was lying on the pallet earlier. It was a sadness that doesn't just disappear—not even with the help of the most magical tea in all China.

And so, though I know it's wrong to lie, that Girl Guides are always supposed to tell the truth, I decide to tell a lie. A big one. Because in the same way that Miss E. has been trying to protect us, I realize that now it's up to me to try to protect her.

I look Miss E. in the eye. I nearly turn away, but I stop myself. I need her to believe what I'm about to tell her. I suck in my breath. "Corporal Hashimoto," I say after I exhale, "escaped."

Miss E. shuts her eyes tight. I don't know what she's imagining, but the dimple in her cheek makes me think it is something wonderful.

"Oh, Gwen," she says, "what excellent news!"

Miss E. pulls me in for a hug.

I feel a twinge of guilt. Lying is wrong. Girl Guides don't lie. But sometimes we have to lie to protect people we love. It's something I learned from Miss E.

The problem with a lie is that a lot can go wrong. If the others hear that Corporal Hashimoto has been killed, I will have to get them to agree not to tell Miss E. And what if Lu hears the news and tells her? Though it feels wonderful to have Miss E.'s arms around me, I am already thinking about all the people I will have to talk to, to make them promise not to share the news of Corporal Hashimoto's fate. I will explain that in a strange reversal of the order of things at Weihsien, it's our turn now to protect Miss E.

"Why don't we sing a song together?" I whisper into the nape of Miss E.'s neck. It's exactly what she would suggest if we needed cheering up.

Miss E. hugs me tighter. "Yes," she says, "let's."

Miss E. picks the song. "*O happy day, that fixed my choice,*" she starts to sing. I recognize the British hymn and sing along. It's a lovely, hopeful tune, and because it's a hymn I know the choice must have something to do with faith. After all the things I've seen in Weihsien, I'm not sure I'm still a believer. But if there *is* a God, I hope He will forgive me for all the things I've done wrong. For having unkind thoughts, for being selfish, for smacking Jeanette, for nearly killing a man and for lying to Miss E.

After the song is over I decide to go to the lending library. That's because Miss E. told me Tilly and Jeanette went there to choose books. I need to tell them what happened to Corporal Hashimoto and how it is now up to us to protect Miss E. I hope they'll play along.

But my friends aren't at the lending library. I also don't run into them on the way over. Since I'm here, I decide I might as well scan the wooden crates to see if there's a book that catches my eye. I can't tell you the kind of book I'm looking for. I only have the feeling that when I spot it, I'll know. I wonder if, in that way, choosing a book from a lending library could be a little like falling in love.

There are several new-old religious tracts. One is called *Treasury of the Christian World*. Another is called *The War Against Sin*. Those are definitely *not* the books I'm in the mood for.

A threadbare navy blue book spine catches my attention. Because the book's title is in blue too, I have to lean in to read it. It's *Around the World in Eighty Days* by Jules Verne.

The books on the shelf are tightly packed together, so I need to tug hard to pull out the book. It's the one Matthew borrowed. I recognize the serious-looking men and women on the cover. I press the book to my chest. It's a little like having Matthew back at Weihsien.

Though I've never been a fan of adventure novels, I decide I'll read it from cover to cover, without skipping a word. Maybe then Matthew won't feel so far away.

I flip through the yellowed pages, and when I do a slip of cardboard falls to the ground.

It's an old library card with columns running across it and several black ink stamps. When I turn it over, my heart skips a beat. It's a message. Though it isn't addressed or signed, I know it's for me and that Matthew wrote it.

I'm sorry for not saying a proper goodbye and for ignoring you in front of the others. You will understand that I had my reasons. Do everything you can to protect the dancer. Perhaps one day we shall meet again. I hope so.

I read the note over and over again, so many times I can say it by heart without looking at it. The dancer is Miss E. So I did the right thing by protecting her from the news of Corporal Hashimoto's death. Even more important, Matthew hopes we'll meet again.

THIRTY-SIX

There won't be a funeral for Mr. Liddell.

"The Japanese have disposed of his body" is all Miss E. will tell us. "May he rest in peace."

"That's probably what they did with Corp—" Tilly begins to say, but then she remembers the promise she made to me, and she stops herself.

"Corporal Hashimoto?" Miss E. asks.

And just like that, the lie I told to protect Miss E. is exposed.

"But I heard," Miss E. says, and she crinkles her forehead the way she does when she's confused, "that Corporal Hashimoto escaped. Gwen"—she spins around to look at me—"you're the one who told me about Corporal Hashimoto."

There's no point denying the lie. "I wanted to protect you." My voice is calm, but my insides are fluttering. What if Miss E. gets angry with me? "I'm terribly sorry."

"Protect me? *Protect me?*" Miss E. has raised her voice. So she *is* angry! "Protect me from *what* exactly?"

"From the truth." I can't think of a better answer. And then I add, "The way you've been protecting us."

Miss E. does not understand my thinking. "I don't need protecting!" She puts her hands on her hips and leans down so she can look into my eyes. "What did they do to Corporal Hashimoto? Tell me! Tell me right now!"

I don't have the heart, or maybe it's that I don't have the courage to tell her what I saw—the signs of a scuffle and Corporal Hashimoto's crumpled body on the floor.

Tilly answers for me. When she speaks her voice is flat and calm. "They tortured him. Then they killed him. Gwen saw the body. She begged us not to tell you."

"Do you mean to say you're all in on this…this *deception?*" I didn't know Miss E.'s eyes could get so wide or that she could get so angry.

Jeanette raises her hand. "For the record," she says, "I was against it. But you know how Gwen is."

"What does that mean?" I ask her.

Jeanette bites her lip.

"Well, what does it mean?"

"Determined," Jeanette says. "You can be very determined, Gwen. And we've all seen what you're like when you lose your temper."

Which goes to show that Jeanette has not totally forgiven me for smacking her.

"Corporal Hashimoto," Miss E. says to herself, shaking her head. "The poor, poor man. I was so hoping he was safe."

"That's why I didn't want you to know," I tell Miss E. "So you could still have hope for Corporal Hashimoto. The way you've given us hope. Even if it isn't always true." My voice breaks. Not only because I'm sorry for the lie and for being caught telling it, but also because I'm beginning to wonder if maybe there really is no hope. All of Miss E.'s songs and games, all of the Girl Guide teachings—what can they do in the end to protect us from evil and death?

"There is *always* hope," Miss E. insists. "It's the one thing no one can take away from us. And if they try, we can't let them. Never, ever."

I wish I could say what happens next is my idea, but it isn't. It's Jeanette's idea—to make our own funeral for Mr. Liddell and Corporal Hashimoto. "And for Albertine," Jeanette adds. "Even if we don't have their bodies."

We join hands and form a circle.

Miss E. is the first to speak. "Thank you, Lord, for giving us Mr. Liddell and Corporal Hashimoto and Albertine. We thank you for all the good they brought into our lives. We ask you to protect their souls." Miss E. is quiet for a moment, and then, without lifting her head to look at us, she says, "You can say whatever you'd like to, Girl Guides. All that matters is that it's *honest*." I know that's a message for me.

"I'm sorry for lying." As soon as I say that, I realize it's not exactly right for a funeral service. But Miss E. said we could say whatever we want to. "There's something else I'm sorry about..."

"I hope you're not going to apologize again for smacking me," Jeanette says.

"She should keep apologizing for it," Cathy says.

"I think she apologized enough," Dot tells her.

This funeral service is getting stranger by the second. I half expect Miss E. to tell us to focus on the loved ones we have lost, but she doesn't.

"It wasn't the smacking I was going to apologize for. It's something else," I say quietly. I cannot look the others in the eye, so I keep my gaze on the ground. "I tried to poison a Japanese soldier. It was the only thing I could think of doing to help save Corporal Hashimoto's life." I try not to sniffle.

Tilly lets go of my hand. "You did?" she says. "That's amazing! How brave of you, Gwen! I didn't know you had it in you!"

"Neither did I." This time I can't help sniffling. "The poison spilled on the floor. But if it hadn't spilled, I might have killed him."

"You *didn't* kill him," Miss E. says. "The Lord protected you—and the soldier too."

"I guess so. But I wish he'd also protected Mr. Liddell and Corporal Hashimoto." It doesn't feel right to include Albertine in this list, so I don't. She gave her life to feed us.

But it seems to me that nothing good came from either Mr. Liddell's or Corporal Hashimoto's death.

I swallow hard. "Mr. Liddell and Corporal Hashimoto, I want to thank you. For setting such good examples. For doing so many good turns. And for being selfless."

"May your souls find peace," Jeanette adds.

Tilly is holding my hand again. "Mr. Liddell and Corporal Hashimoto, I want to say I'm sorry you two didn't get a real funeral. I hope we've made up for that a little bit today."

Jeanette nudges Miss E. "Could you do a pirouette?" she asks her.

"A pirouette? At a funeral?" Miss E. sounds surprised, but I can see her dimples showing.

It's an unusual ending for an unusual funeral. Miss E. doesn't *do* a pirouette. Instead she decides to teach us how to do the move. She says it will take lots of practice before we're good at it. But that there are some tricks. "A pirouette requires a lot of courage." Miss E. looks at me when she says this. I think she is telling me that even if I've made mistakes, she thinks I'm courageous.

"The dancer has to stay open—and lifted," Miss E. continues.

Tilly throws back her shoulders and lifts her chest. "Like this?" she asks.

"Exactly. Very nice, Matilda," Miss E. tells her.

The rest of us throw back our shoulders and lift our chests exactly the way Tilly did.

"You can't expect to get the pirouette right on your very first try," Miss E. says. "Like everything good and important, learning to do a pirouette takes many tries. Hundreds, thousands even! But not a single one of those tries will be wasted."

Tilly doesn't wait for Miss E. to finish her lesson. Instead she tries to do a pirouette. When she loses her footing and stumbles, she laughs.

Jeanette tries it too. But she says it makes her dizzy.

"There's a trick for that too," Miss E. explains. "You need to focus on one point. Even when the world is whirling around you like a top, keep that one point always in your mind. And always, always keep your chin up." She points to her own chin and raises it a half inch.

Keep your chin up.

It's the first time Miss E. has told us that. It makes perfect sense coming from her. But I've heard those words many, many times. Why did I never think of them before? *Keep your chin up.* My mother said it to me every morning after breakfast. It was also the last thing she said to me when she and my father left me at the boarding school in Chefoo.

I will keep my chin up.

Not just when I practice my pirouettes—but always.

Trying to be positive can't fix everything. Sometimes *not* looking at the negatives causes problems too. But trying to be positive, trying to keep my chin up…well, I think I'd rather live that way.

THIRTY-SEVEN

There's been peace in Europe since just after our make-shift funeral in May. Now it is August, and we are still prisoners at Weihsien—caught in a kind of limbo. Our Japanese captors are nervous. They know the end is coming. But they're also afraid of the Chinese guerrillas communists who are sworn enemies of the Japanese.

Miss E. says we must be patient. "It won't be much longer," she promises. "I feel it in my bones."

"What about the communists? Do you think they'll come and set us free?" Jeanette asks Miss E.

Tilly snorts. "Haven't you heard, Jeanette? The commies have already been to Weihsien, only not to set us free. Just to steal our food!"

"Is that true?" Jeanette asks Miss E.

For a change, Miss E. doesn't avoid the question. "I'm afraid," she says quietly, "that Matilda is right."

"What if we die in here?" I ask.

"We won't," Miss E. says. "I promise you we won't."

"You can't promise a thing like that," Tilly snaps.

"I can," Miss E. answers.

We wait until Miss E. leaves to continue the conversation. Since the news of the end of the war in Europe, we've been getting even less to eat. Some of the women are making soup from bones and rotten vegetables. Miss E. has gone to help them.

We haven't bothered with work detail in weeks. The Japanese soldiers are too worried about what will happen to them if they lose this war to bother enforcing rules or getting angry with us. Miss E. will insist we have our daily lesson, but in the meantime we lie on our sleeping pallets and chat, stopping now and then to swat a louse.

"If we do die here," I say to the other girls, "what will be left of us?"

Tilly, who is next to me, shakes her head. "Nothing," she says, looking up at the ceiling. "Nothing will be left of us—besides our bones and teeth."

"We should leave something," I say.

"Like what?" Dot asks.

"Like…I don't know…a message in a bottle."

"That's for people who are lost at sea," Cathy says.

"We're lost on land," Tilly says.

"What if we all sign our names?" I suggest. "So the world knows we were here." I pause. "In case."

So even though we are too weak to do much more than lie on the sleeping pallets, we get up and write our names on the inside of the door to our hut. Twenty-eight names for twenty-eight girls. It's a miracle that we are all still together. We could never have made it this long without Miss E.

When she gets back I'll ask her to add her name to our list.

We are so used to the noises of Weihsien—the barking dogs, the shouting Japanese soldiers, the bells for roll call, even the sounds our hands make when we slap a louse or a bedbug—that we all turn to each other when we hear a droning mechanical sound overhead, coming from outside.

An airplane!

Can it really be an airplane?

"Do you think it's the guerrillas? That they've come to kidnap us?" Eunice asks.

"The guerrillas don't have food. How do you expect them to have a plane?" Tilly asks. She tugs on my hand. Though it's sweltering hot in our hut and even hotter outside, Tilly's hand feels ice cold. It's from not getting enough to eat. "Let's go see what's going on."

All twenty-eight of us go to stand outside our hut. The grounds are thick with other prisoners doing the same thing as us—peering up into the sky. The droning sound comes closer. And now a silver airplane is circling overhead. "It's a B-24," a voice calls out. "An American B-24!"

"An American B-24!" Everyone seems to be calling this out at the same time. "An American B-24!"

I am standing between Jeanette and Tilly. The three of us fall into each other's arms. But it's hard to hug your friends when you are all jumping up and down. Other girls are dancing. Some prisoners are weeping. And here comes Miss E.—she's doing a pirouette!

And then the most incredible thing happens—a white parachute drops down from the underbelly of the airplane. Then there are more white parachutes. Seven in all. It's like watching clouds fall from the sky. The Americans have come to set us free!

Prisoners sing victory songs. Prisoners run over to the soldiers—hugging and kissing them. Tilly, Jeanette and I run over to the nearest parachute. Prisoners are helping to untangle an American soldier from the parachute's cords.

"Did you bring food for us?" Tilly calls out. "We're starving!"

The soldier has heard Tilly's question even if he can't see her. "Food is coming!" he promises.

"Dr. McGregor! Get Dr. McGregor right away!" voices call from the field where several of the parachutes have landed.

"What's going on?"

"This soldier's hurt his leg. I think it's broken!" someone calls out.

Dr. McGregor is hobbling down the path, looking more old and tired than ever, but smiling like a boy on Christmas morning. The small crowd in the field makes room for him to crouch down and treat his patient.

Word spreads quickly about the upcoming food delivery. It won't arrive until tomorrow, when there will be more B-24s. These ones will drop canisters of food, clothing, cigarettes and chocolate.

"Did you hear we're getting chocolate?"

"And Lucky Strike cigarettes!"

Miss E. is as excited as we are. "We're going to skip our lesson for today!" she announces, but no one is really listening. She claps her hands. "Girl Guides!" she says. "We have work to do. We need to make a giant sign for the pilots flying overhead tomorrow. We need to let them know where it's safe to drop the canisters."

"What will we use to make a giant sign?" Cathy asks.

I look out at all the action going on around me. That's when the answer comes to me. "A parachute!" I tell the others.

"Of course!" Miss E. says. She reaches out to squeeze my hand. "Honestly, Gwen, I don't know what we'd do without you!"

THIRTY-EIGHT

We use every pen and pencil and even some old shoe polish to write the words *OK TO LAND* in giant black letters on one of the parachutes.

Early in the morning we lay our sign on the eggplant field. Though I'm as hungry as I was yesterday, I haven't felt this energetic since...well, I can't remember the last time I felt this way. Any moment now those canisters with food will be arriving. Oh, the thought of a square of chocolate melting on my tongue is almost too much to bear.

"Here comes a plane!" someone calls out. It's another B-24, and there are more to follow.

The girls from my hut jump up and down. We point toward our sign. Several metal canisters drop down from the first airplane and land smack in the middle of the eggplant field. The pilot must have seen our sign.

"Yay!" we shout—because our sign worked and because we're finally, finally going to get real food to eat.

We all rush toward the field. "No! No! No! Absolutely no!" Miss E. shouts. At first we don't listen, but then she calls out after us, her voice hoarse from shouting, "It's too dangerous. You could get hit by one of those canisters."

And so we go back and wait outside our hut for the moment when Miss E. tells us it is safe to leave.

Just then there is a terrible crash. We hear voices shouting, "What is it?" "What happened?" and "What in God's name was that noise?"

One of the pilots didn't see our sign. He dumped a giant wooden crate over the main kitchen, and it has made a hole in the roof.

"Let's go see what was in that crate!" Tilly calls out.

Miss E.'s eyes flash. "I told you—absolutely NOT! In fact, Girl Guides, I insist you take cover until I tell you it's safe to come out. Back to the hut this instant! On the double, Girl Guides!"

What comes next feels like the longest half hour of our lives. "How much longer do you think it will be?" Jeanette asks.

"How should I know?" Tilly says.

"What do you think, Gwen?"

"I'm sure it won't be much longer," I tell Jeanette.

When we can no longer hear the drone of airplane engines, Tilly announces that she can't handle any more waiting around. "Let's go," she says.

"Miss E. told us to wait until she came back to tell us the coast was clear," I say to Tilly.

Tilly looks me right in the eye. "The coast *is* clear," she says. I know what she's doing. She's asking me to go against Miss E.'s wishes. To be my own person—the way Tilly is and always has been her own person. Tilly seems to know what I'm thinking because she says, "She won't always be there to look after us or to tell us what to do. Now that the Americans have come, we'll be sent back to our own families." Tilly gulps, and in that moment I understand I'm not the only one who has mixed feelings about returning to my family.

What will I have in common with my parents? Miss E. is the closest thing I've had to a parent in nearly three years. If only there were a way for all of us to stay together.

"Girl Guides!" It's Miss E. She wants us to follow her. She says there are tins and tins of Spam and that we can each start with a spoonful. The wooden crate that made a hole in the kitchen roof was full of canned peaches. We can have those for dessert.

"Is there chocolate?" Cathy and Dot want to know.

"The chocolate is for later," Miss E. says.

The Spam is delicious. It's hard to believe that there is more Spam, and other good things to eat, and chocolate. We won't have to starve anymore. What will I think about? I have spent so much time these last years thinking about my empty stomach.

A crowd gathers by the guardhouse. That's where I saw Corporal Hashimoto's body at the back of the small cell.

"Let's see what's going on!" Eunice suggests.

There's the camp commander. The last time I saw him was when he stomped on Miss E.'s reading glasses. He is handing over his sword to an American soldier.

"That's Major Stanley Staiger," someone whispers. "They call him the 'flying ace.'"

We gather around to watch what feels like an important historical moment.

Major Staiger pushes the sword away from him. Why is he doing that?

"I don't want your sword," Major Staiger tells the commander. But he says it loudly, and we know it's because he wants us all to hear him. An interpreter repeats Major Staiger's words in Japanese. "Besides, you'll be needing your sword," Major Staiger continues. We all gasp when he says that.

"On behalf of the United States Army, I hereby order you to defend Weihsien and all of its inhabitants—every single one—against guerrillas and looters."

The commander bows low to Major Staiger. "Thank you," he says.

The men who were our captors are now our defenders. Soon the Americans and the Chinese authorities will find a way to return us to our families. Everything feels upside down. I don't know if my life will ever feel right side up again.

Then I think of something Miss E. taught us: to focus on a fixed point when the world is whirling like a top. I look up at the watchtower.

I will always remember the afternoon Corporal Hashimoto led Tilly and me in that direction, and how scared we were. I will always remember how he lifted us up so we could see over the electrified wall.

Most of all, I will always remember the sight of a world without walls and the feeling of freedom it gave me. The feeling that I could go anywhere, be anyone and do anything. Wherever life takes me, I will do my best to hold on to that feeling.

AUTHOR'S NOTE

Much has been written about the Second World War. Most literature about this period is set in Europe. That includes my own historical novel, *What World Is Left* (Orca 2008), which was based on my mother's childhood experience in a Nazi concentration camp in what is now the Czech Republic. But the war was also fought on another continent. And as in all wars, innocent children often ended up suffering.

In Asia thousands of children spent the war imprisoned in Japanese internment camps. One was called the Weihsien Civilian Assembly Center. Originally built as an American Presbyterian mission, Weihsien became a place of unrelenting misery. There was not enough food, diseases like dysentery were rampant, and in addition to doing forced labor, prisoners—even those who were very young— were routinely beaten. Among the prisoners at Weihsien were some 140 students from a boarding school in Chefoo and their teachers. The teachers came up with an unusual plan: to encourage their young charges to follow the Girl Guide Code of Conduct. By doing so, the teachers hoped to raise the children's spirits and to protect them from the harsh reality of imprisonment.

Although, as I've explained in my acknowledgments, Mary Previte was not available for an interview, she did share some of her thoughts about Weihsien in an email message to me. Mary gave her permission for me to quote her words: *What story wakes people up these days? Even in a wartime internment camp, children and God's humble people turn a very ugly world into one where goodness triumphs over evil. How beautiful is that?...We children/students were blessed by our teachers who anchored us. Separated from our parents by warring armies, most of us were separated from our parents for five or more years. So our Chefoo boarding school teachers were our substitute parents. My...faith and hope [were] ignited by these missionary teachers who were also prisoners. Grown-ups turned challenges into games.*

The Girl Guide Code focuses on positive thinking and putting others first. As an author and also as a person known for her sunny disposition, I wanted to explore what it means to be cheerful. Can a positive attitude help us deal with challenging situations? And, just as important, can cheerfulness sometimes get us into trouble by preventing us from seeing the truth? I've grappled with these questions while writing this book.

There were both Girl Guides and Girl Scouts at Weihsein. The Girl Guide movement originated in Europe in 1909; the Girl Scout movement began three years later in the United States. Because my Miss E. is British, I chose to use Girl Guides in this story.

A final word: the children in my story use the word *coolies* when they refer to the Chinese laborers who work inside Weihsien. Now considered a racial slur, the term dates back to the nineteenth century and was commonly used in India, China and Asia to describe laborers.

RESOURCES

Print

Farrell, Mary Cronk. *Pure Grit: How American World War II Nurses Survived Battle and Prison Camp in the Pacific.* New York, NY: Abrams, 2014.

Monahan, Evelyn M., and Rosemary Neidel-Greenlee. *All This Hell: U.S. Nurses Imprisoned by the Japanese.* Lexington, KY: University Press of Kentucky, 2000.

Tyrer, Nicola. *Stolen Childhoods: The Untold Story of the Children Interned by the Japanese in the Second World War.* London, UK: Weidenfeld & Nicolson, 2011.

Online

Association for Diplomatic Studies & Training. "Moments in U.S. Diplomatic History: Escape from Japanese Internment in China." https://adst.org/2015/11/escape-from-japanese-internment-in-china/#.WnDTfEusNAY.

"Captain's Log." *This American Life*, episode 559, June 26, 2015. Public radio podcast. thisamericanlife.org/559/captains-log.

Girl Scouts of the United States of America. "Traditions." girlscouts.org/en/about-girl-scouts/traditions.html.

Nussbaum, Debra. "In Person; She Teaches Survival, Learned the Hard Way." *New York Times*, Dec. 31, 2000. nytimes.com/2000/12/31/nyregion/in-person-she-teaches-survival-learned-the-hard-way.html?pagewanted=all.

Previte, Mary Taylor. "A Song of Salvation at Weihsien Prison Camp." August 25, 1985. weihsien-paintings.org/Mprevite/inquirer/MPrevite.htm.

ACKNOWLEDGMENTS

On June 26, 2015, my friend (and editor) Sarah Harvey called and told me to turn on the radio. She was listening to an episode of *This American Life*, a public radio program. The episode, called "Cookies and Monsters," told the story of a remarkable Girl Guide troop at the Weihsien Civilian Assembly Center in China during the Second World War. Following the Girl Guide Code of Conduct and maintaining a positive attitude helped these children survive a harrowing ordeal. "You have to write a book about this," Sarah told me. So I did. I managed to track down Mary Previte, one of the Girl Guides who survived Weihsien, and whose story was featured in the radio broadcast. Though Mary was not available for an interview with me, I owe her a great debt, since her account was the inspiration for this book. Many thanks to Sarah for encouraging me to imagine life at the internment camp and for helping me get deeper into my story. Thanks to the rest of the team at Orca for being wonderful. Thanks to Dwight McIntyre for answering my questions about slaughtering a pig. Finally, thanks to my friend Leanne Kinsella for loving this story as much as I do.

Monique Polak is the author of more than twenty novels for kids and young adults. She has also written two nonfiction books for kids (*Passover: Festival of Freedom* and *I Am a Feminist: Claiming the F-Word in Turbulent Times*), as well as a board book for toddlers. Monique is a two-time winner of the Quebec Writers' Federation Prize for Children's and Young Adult Fiction. In addition to being an active freelance journalist whose work appears regularly in the *Montreal Gazette*, Monique teaches English literature, creative writing and humanities at Marianopolis College in Montreal, Quebec. For more information, visit moniquepolak.com.